D1170740

Disney · PIXAR
FINDING NEMO

SCRIPT ADAPTATION
Charles Bazaldua

LAYOUT / PENCIL / INK
Claudio Sciarrone

COLOR
Gabriella Matta, Davide Baldoni

ART OPTIMIZATION
Dario Calabria

COVER LAYOUT / PENCIL / INK
Claudio Sciarrone

COVER COLOR
Gabriella Matta, Davide Baldoni

ABDOBOOKS.COM

Reinforced library bound edition published in 2021 by Spotlight, a division of ABDO, PO Box 398166, Minneapolis, Minnesota 55439. Spotlight produces high-quality reinforced library bound editions for schools and libraries. Published by agreement with Disney Enterprises, Inc.

Printed in the United States of America, North Mankato, Minnesota.
042020
092020

THIS BOOK CONTAINS
RECYCLED MATERIALS

Library of Congress Control Number: 2020932996

Publisher's Cataloging-in-Publication Data

Names: Bazaldua, Charles, author. | Sciarrone, Claudio, illustrator.
Title: Finding Nemo / by Charles Bazaldua; illustrated by Claudio Sciarrone.
Description: Minneapolis, Minnesota: Spotlight, 2021. | Series: Disney and Pixar movies
Summary: When his son Nemo is kidnapped, Marlin teams up with Dory to cross the ocean to get his son back.
Identifiers: ISBN 9781532145490 (lib. bdg.)
Subjects: LCSH: Finding Nemo (Motion picture)--Juvenile fiction. | Fishes--Juvenile fiction. | Coral reef animals--Juvenile fiction. | Parent and child--Juvenile fiction. | Adventure stories--Juvenile fiction. | Graphic novels--Juvenile fiction.
Classification: DDC 741.5--dc23

Spotlight

A Division of ABDO
abdobooks.com

ON THE EDGE OF THE GREAT BARRIER REEF, CORAL AND MARLIN, A PAIR OF CLOWNFISH, GAZE HAPPILY AT THEIR YOUNG FAMILY...
WE STILL HAVE TO NAME THEM. I LIKE NEMO.
NEMO? WELL, WE'LL NAME ONE NEMO, BUT I'D LIKE MOST OF THEM TO BE MARLIN, JR...
LIFE SEEMS GOOD TO CAREFREE, HAPPY MARLIN, AS HE PLAYFULLY TEASES CORAL.
THEN, DISASTER STRIKES!
DESPITE MARLIN'S HEROIC ATTEMPT TO SAVE HER...
BONK
TWACK
THE GROTTO IS EMPTY...
CORAL! CORAL! NO! CORAL!
ALL THAT REMAINS OF MARLIN'S FAMILY IS ONE, SMALL, DAMAGED EGG.
I PROMISE I WILL NEVER LET ANYTHING HAPPEN TO YOU, NEMO.

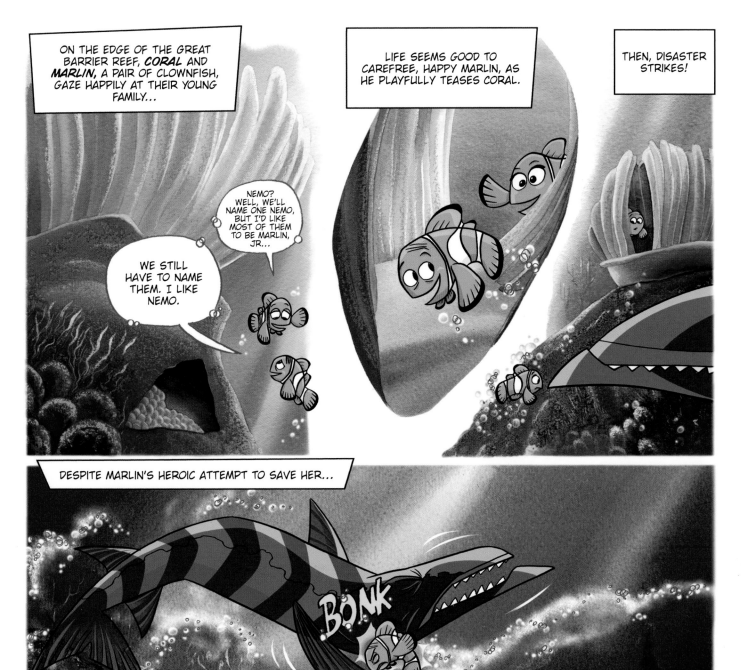

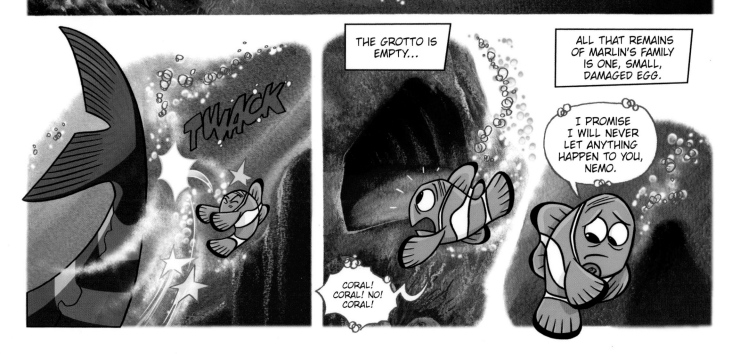

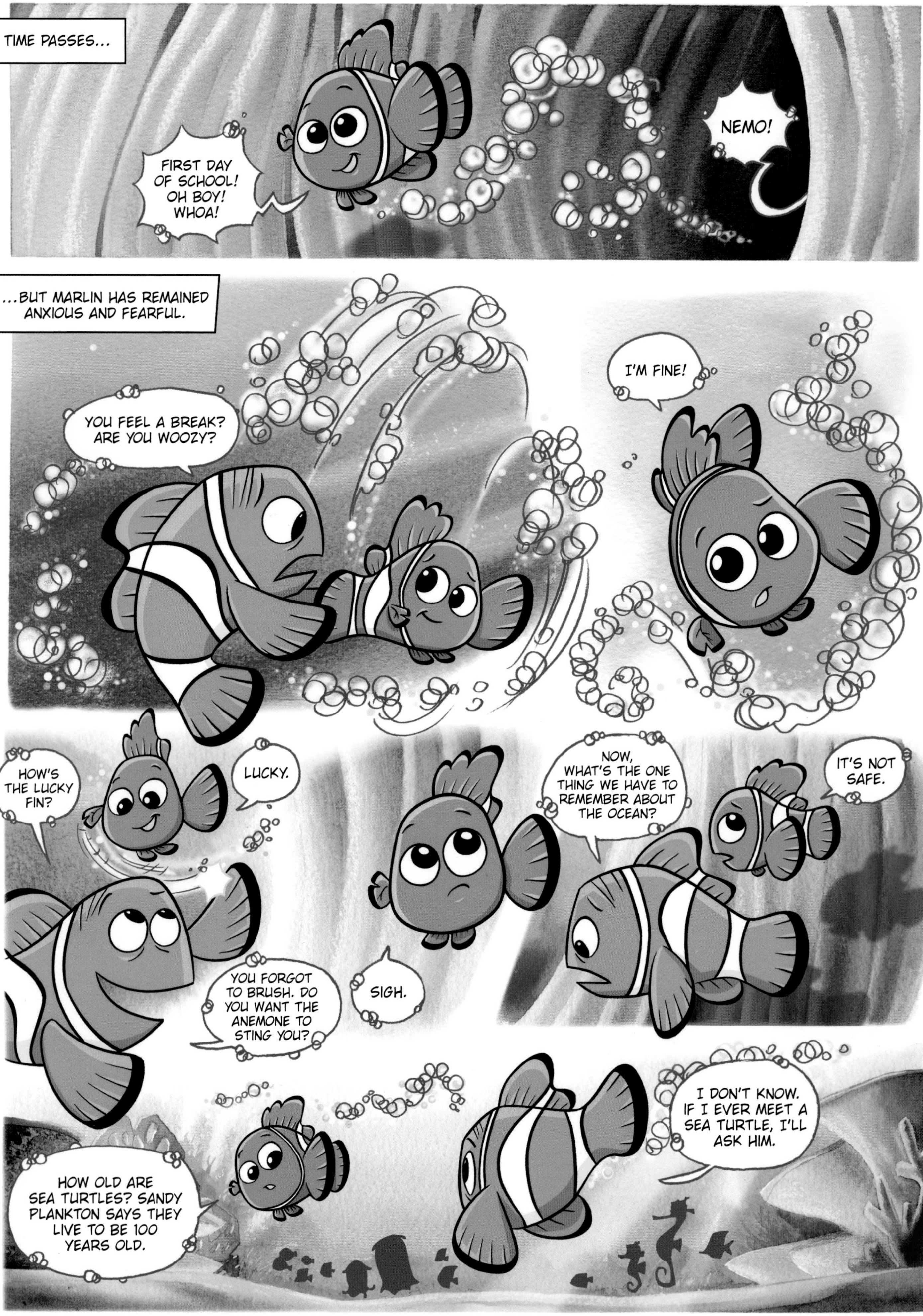

TIME PASSES...
FIRST DAY OF SCHOOL! OH BOY! WHOA!
NEMO!
...BUT MARLIN HAS REMAINED ANXIOUS AND FEARFUL.
YOU FEEL A BREAK? ARE YOU WOOZY?
I'M FINE!
HOW'S THE LUCKY FIN?
LUCKY.
YOU FORGOT TO BRUSH. DO YOU WANT THE ANEMONE TO STING YOU?
SIGH.
NOW, WHAT'S THE ONE THING WE HAVE TO REMEMBER ABOUT THE OCEAN?
IT'S NOT SAFE.
HOW OLD ARE SEA TURTLES? SANDY PLANKTON SAYS THEY LIVE TO BE 100 YEARS OLD.
I DON'T KNOW. IF I EVER MEET A SEA TURTLE, I'LL ASK HIM.

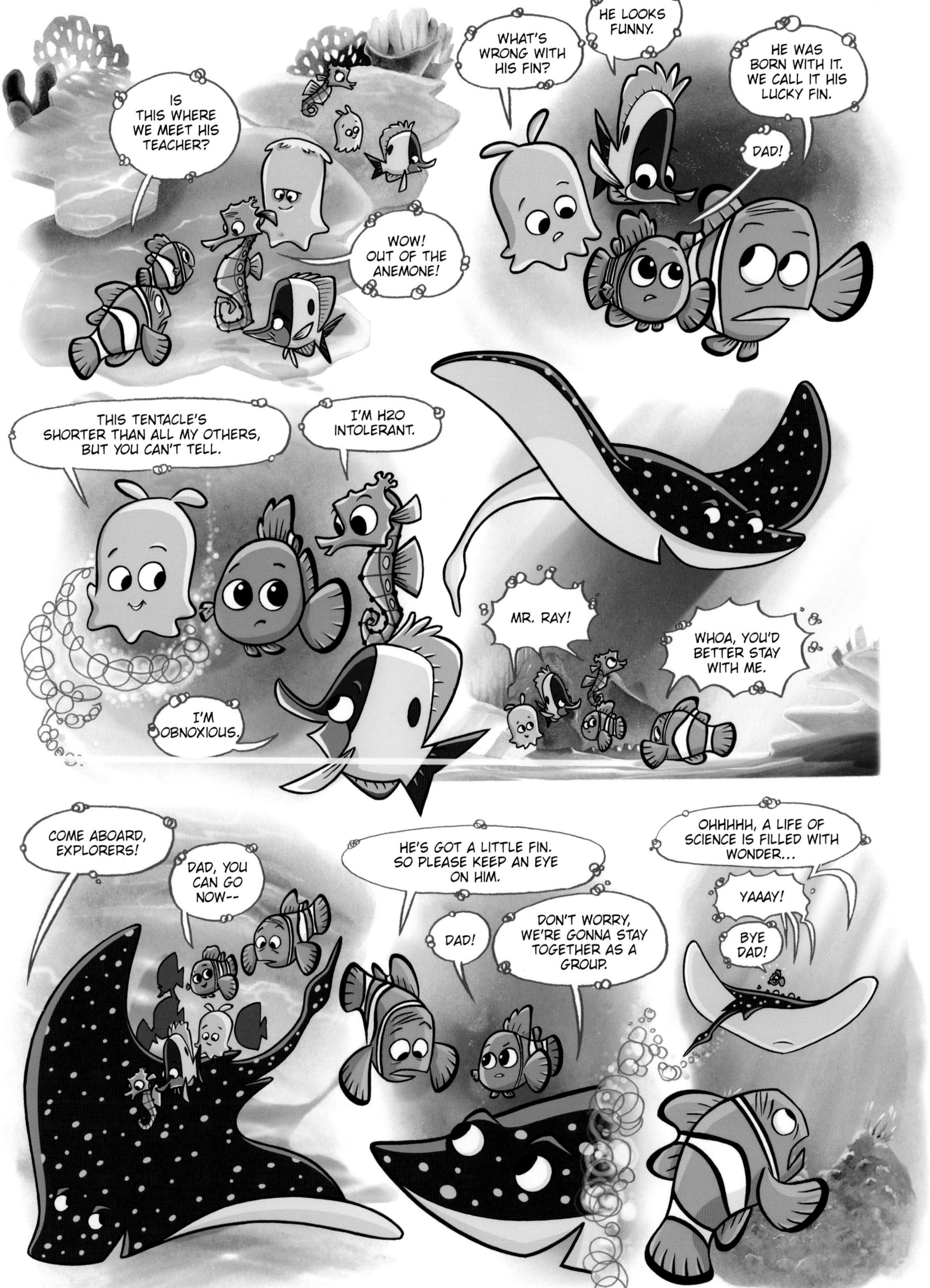

IS THIS WHERE WE MEET HIS TEACHER?
WOW! OUT OF THE ANEMONE!
WHAT'S WRONG WITH HIS FIN?
HE LOOKS FUNNY.
HE WAS BORN WITH IT. WE CALL IT HIS LUCKY FIN.
DAD!
THIS TENTACLE'S SHORTER THAN ALL MY OTHERS, BUT YOU CAN'T TELL.
I'M H2O INTOLERANT.
I'M OBNOXIOUS.
MR. RAY!
WHOA, YOU'D BETTER STAY WITH ME.
COME ABOARD, EXPLORERS!
DAD, YOU CAN GO NOW--
HE'S GOT A LITTLE FIN. SO PLEASE KEEP AN EYE ON HIM.
DAD!
DON'T WORRY, WE'RE GONNA STAY TOGETHER AS A GROUP.
OHHHHH, A LIFE OF SCIENCE IS FILLED WITH WONDER...
YAAAY!
BYE DAD!

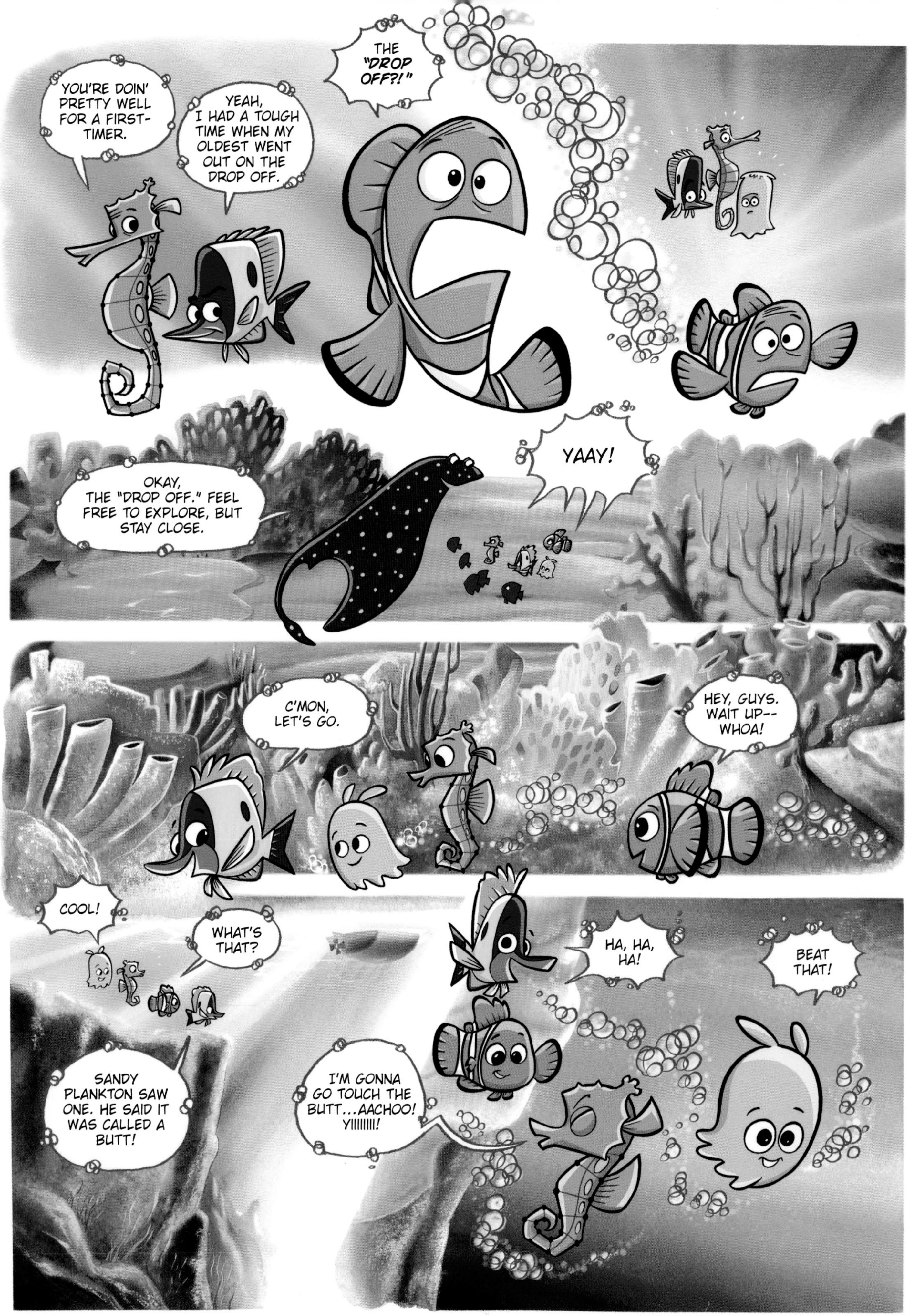

YOU'RE DOIN' PRETTY WELL FOR A FIRST-TIMER.
YEAH, I HAD A TOUGH TIME WHEN MY OLDEST WENT OUT ON THE DROP OFF.
THE *"DROP OFF?!"*
OKAY, THE "DROP OFF." FEEL FREE TO EXPLORE, BUT STAY CLOSE.
YAAY!
C'MON, LET'S GO.
HEY, GUYS. WAIT UP--WHOA!
COOL!
WHAT'S THAT?
SANDY PLANKTON SAW ONE. HE SAID IT WAS CALLED A BUTT!
HA, HA, HA!
BEAT THAT!
I'M GONNA GO TOUCH THE BUTT...AACHOO! YIIIIIIII!

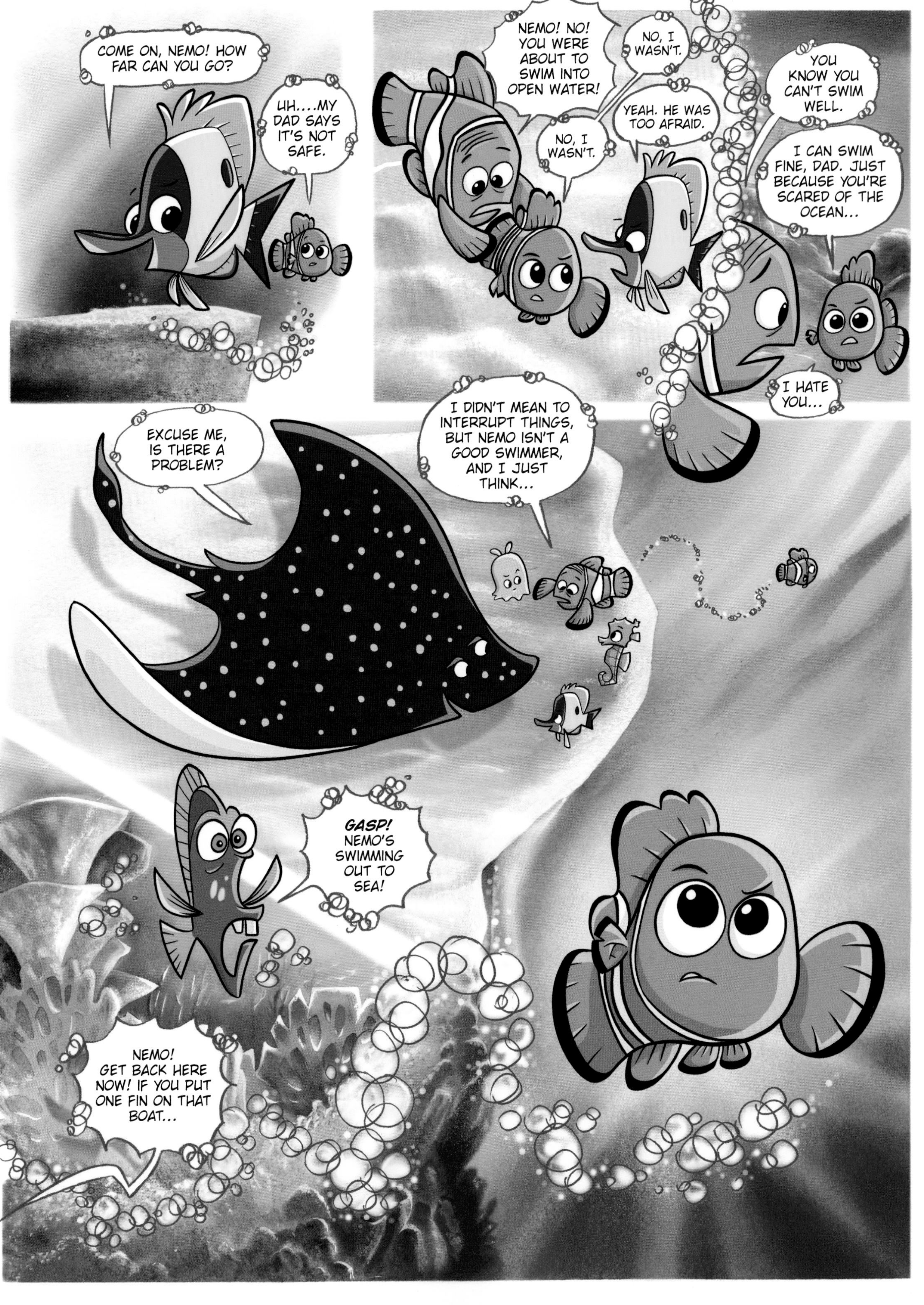

COME ON, NEMO! HOW FAR CAN YOU GO?
UH....MY DAD SAYS IT'S NOT SAFE.
NEMO! NO! YOU WERE ABOUT TO SWIM INTO OPEN WATER!
NO, I WASN'T.
NO, I WASN'T.
YEAH. HE WAS TOO AFRAID.
YOU KNOW YOU CAN'T SWIM WELL.
I CAN SWIM FINE, DAD. JUST BECAUSE YOU'RE SCARED OF THE OCEAN...
I HATE YOU...
EXCUSE ME, IS THERE A PROBLEM?
I DIDN'T MEAN TO INTERRUPT THINGS, BUT NEMO ISN'T A GOOD SWIMMER, AND I JUST THINK...
GASP! NEMO'S SWIMMING OUT TO SEA!
NEMO! GET BACK HERE NOW! IF YOU PUT ONE FIN ON THAT BOAT...

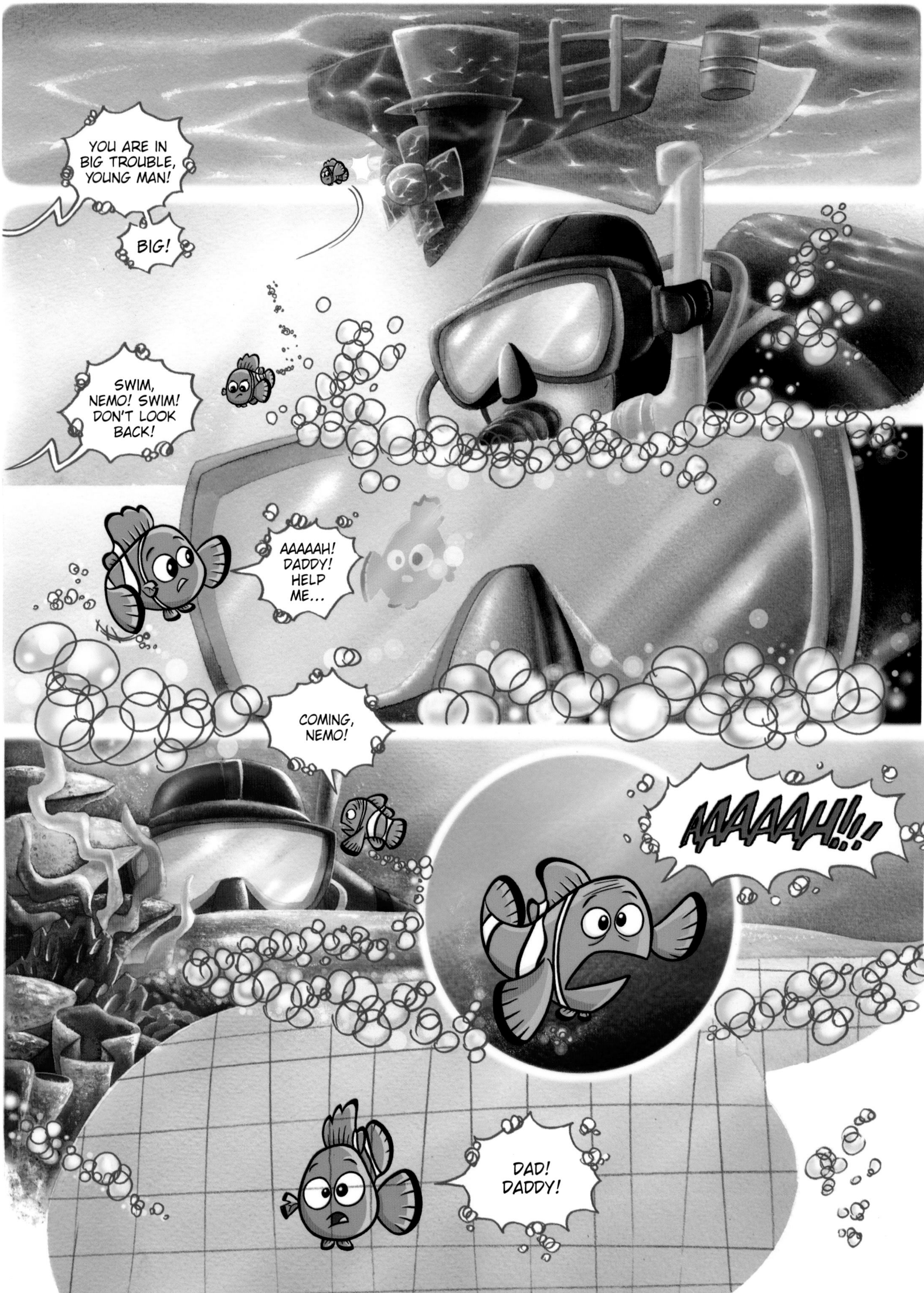
YOU ARE IN BIG TROUBLE, YOUNG MAN!
BIG!
SWIM, NEMO! SWIM! DON'T LOOK BACK!
AAAAAH! DADDY! HELP ME...
COMING, NEMO!
AAAAAH!!!
DAD! DADDY!

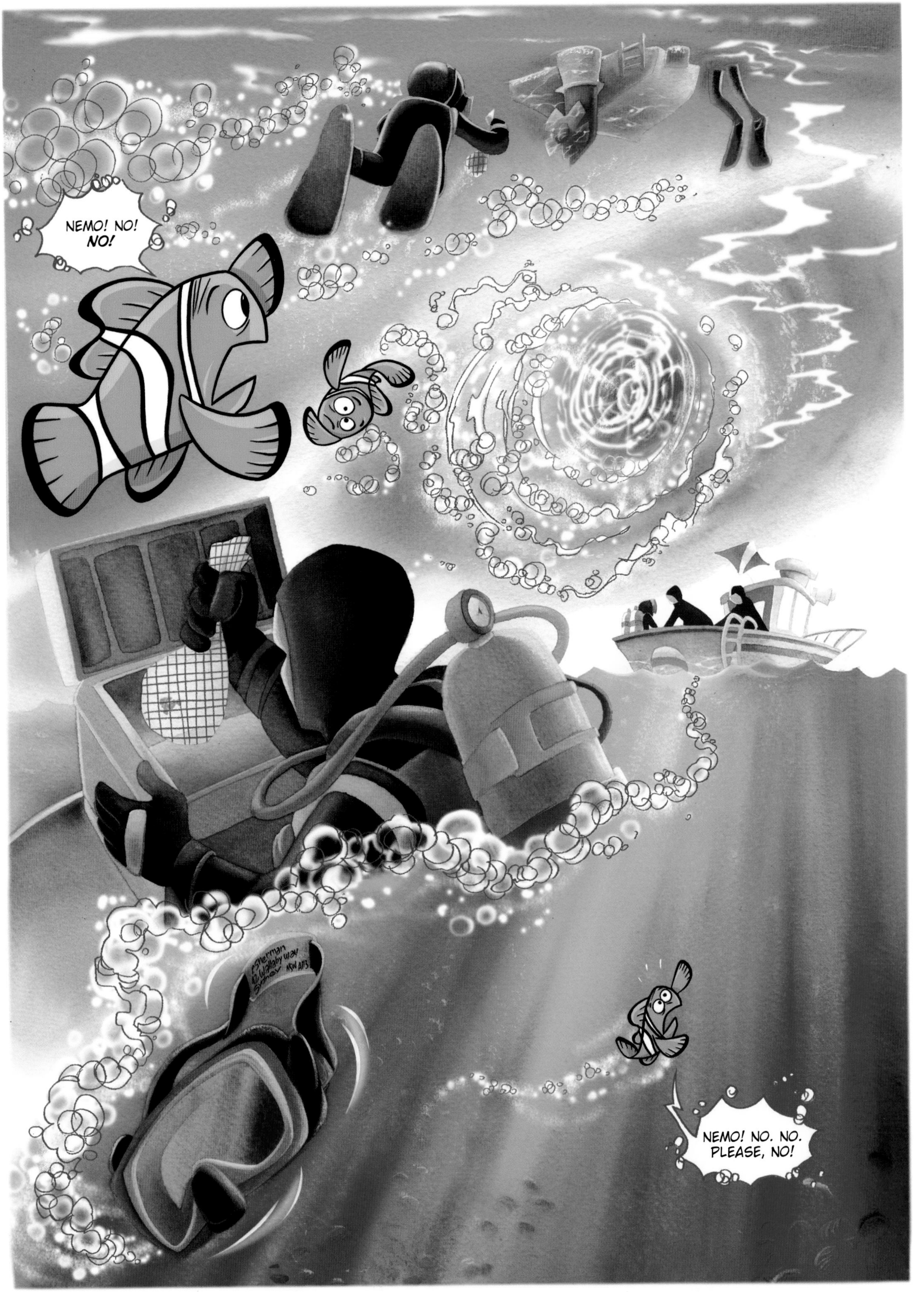
NEMO! NO! NO!
Sherman
42 Wallaby way
Sydney NSW
NEMO! NO. NO. PLEASE, NO!

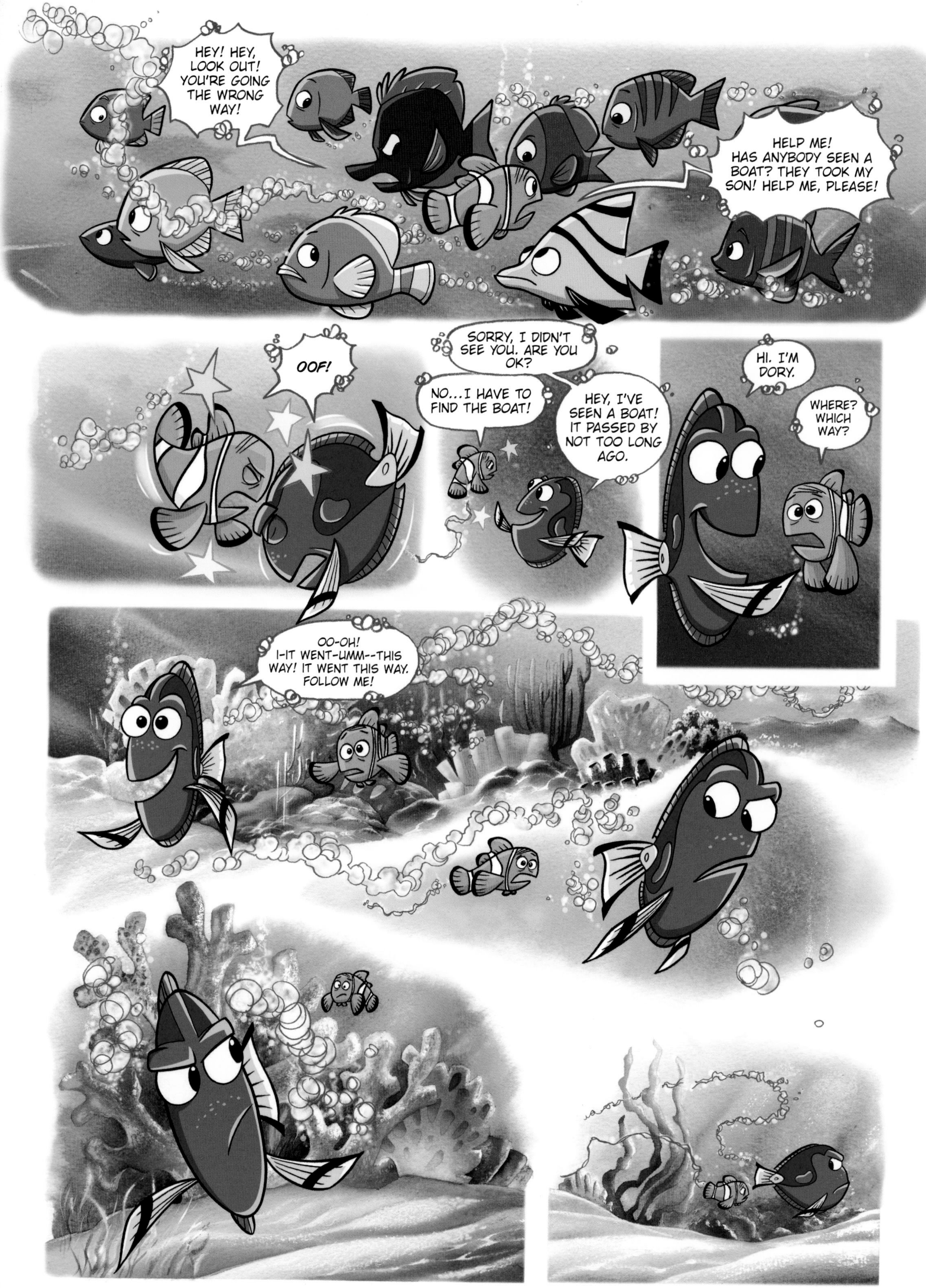
HEY! HEY, LOOK OUT! YOU'RE GOING THE WRONG WAY!
HELP ME! HAS ANYBODY SEEN A BOAT? THEY TOOK MY SON! HELP ME, PLEASE!
OOF!
SORRY, I DIDN'T SEE YOU. ARE YOU OK?
NO...I HAVE TO FIND THE BOAT!
HEY, I'VE SEEN A BOAT! IT PASSED BY NOT TOO LONG AGO.
HI. I'M DORY.
WHERE? WHICH WAY?
OO-OH! I-IT WENT-UMM--THIS WAY! IT WENT THIS WAY. FOLLOW ME!

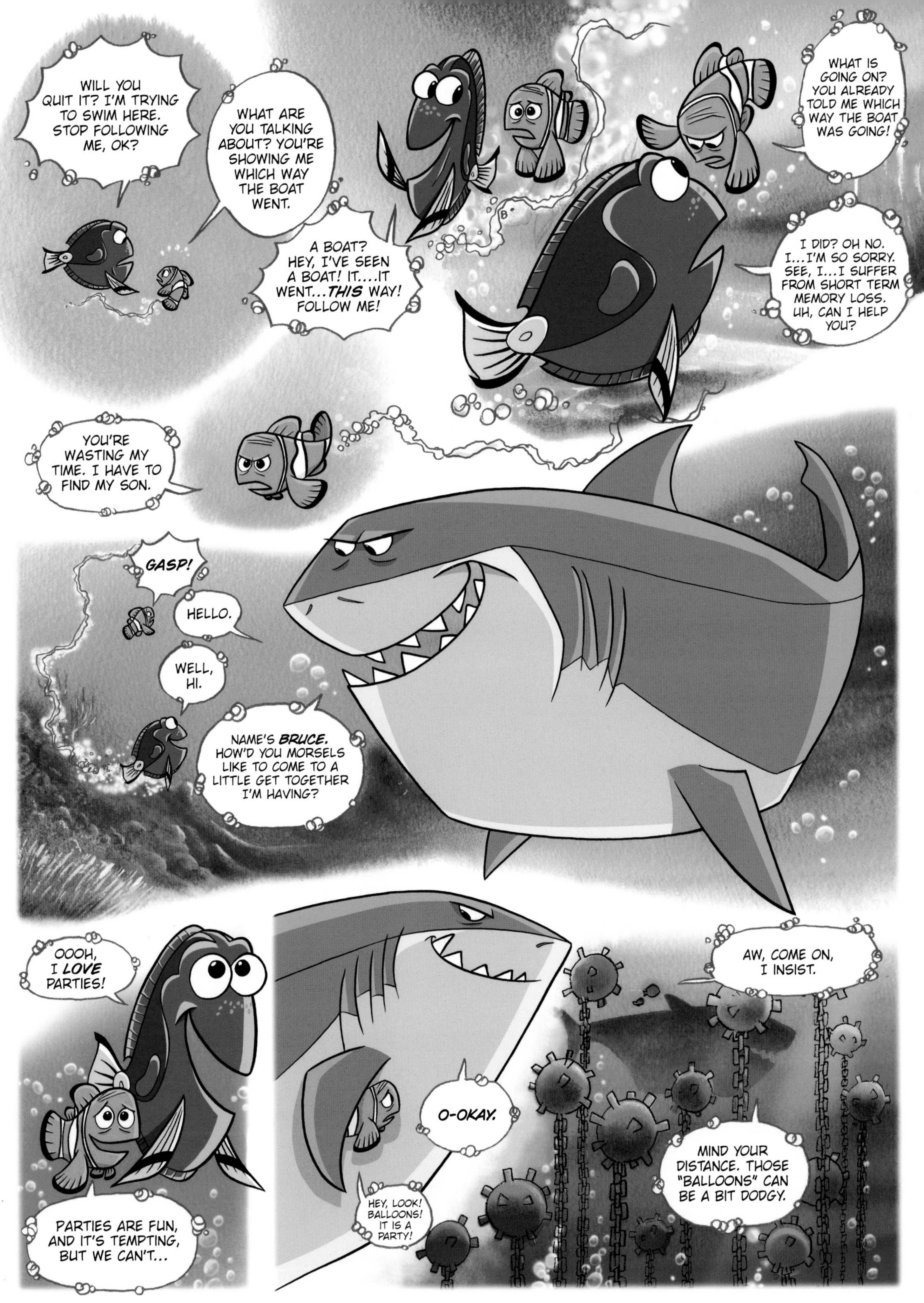
WILL YOU QUIT IT? I'M TRYING TO SWIM HERE. STOP FOLLOWING ME, OK?
WHAT ARE YOU TALKING ABOUT? YOU'RE SHOWING ME WHICH WAY THE BOAT WENT.
A BOAT? HEY, I'VE SEEN A BOAT! IT....IT WENT...*THIS* WAY! FOLLOW ME!
WHAT IS GOING ON? YOU ALREADY TOLD ME WHICH WAY THE BOAT WAS GOING!
I DID? OH NO. I...I'M SO SORRY. SEE, I...I SUFFER FROM SHORT TERM MEMORY LOSS. UH, CAN I HELP YOU?
YOU'RE WASTING MY TIME. I HAVE TO FIND MY SON.
GASP!
HELLO.
WELL, HI.
NAME'S *BRUCE.* HOW'D YOU MORSELS LIKE TO COME TO A LITTLE GET TOGETHER I'M HAVING?
OOOH, I *LOVE* PARTIES!
PARTIES ARE FUN, AND IT'S TEMPTING, BUT WE CAN'T...
AW, COME ON, I INSIST.
O-OKAY.
HEY, LOOK! BALLOONS! IT IS A PARTY!
MIND YOUR DISTANCE. THOSE "BALLOONS" CAN BE A BIT DODGY.

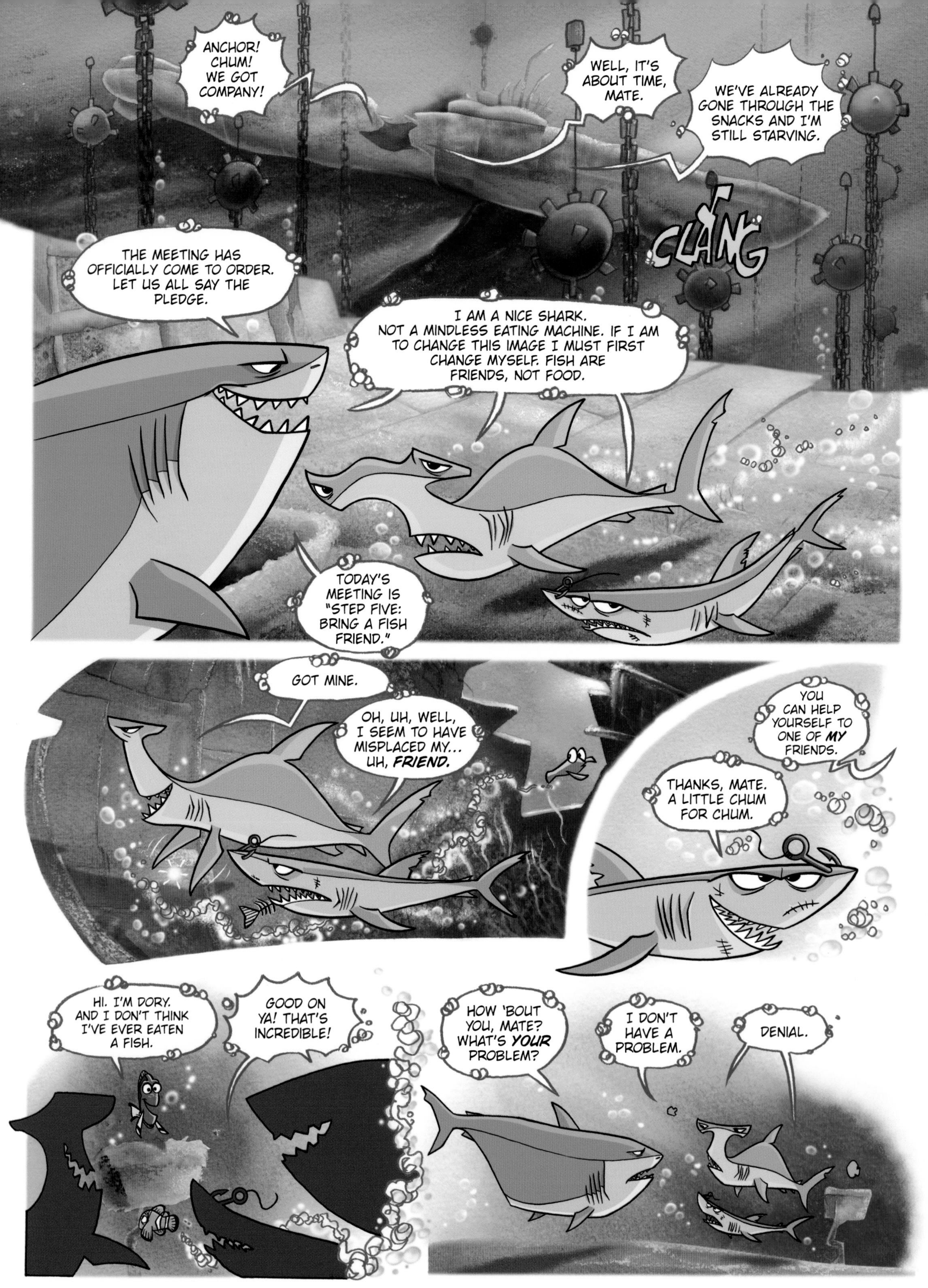

ANCHOR! CHUM! WE GOT COMPANY!
WELL, IT'S ABOUT TIME, MATE.
WE'VE ALREADY GONE THROUGH THE SNACKS AND I'M STILL STARVING.
CLANG
THE MEETING HAS OFFICIALLY COME TO ORDER. LET US ALL SAY THE PLEDGE.
I AM A NICE SHARK. NOT A MINDLESS EATING MACHINE. IF I AM TO CHANGE THIS IMAGE I MUST FIRST CHANGE MYSELF. FISH ARE FRIENDS, NOT FOOD.
TODAY'S MEETING IS "STEP FIVE: BRING A FISH FRIEND."
GOT MINE.
OH, UH, WELL, I SEEM TO HAVE MISPLACED MY... UH, *FRIEND.*
YOU CAN HELP YOURSELF TO ONE OF ***MY*** FRIENDS.
THANKS, MATE. A LITTLE CHUM FOR CHUM.
HI. I'M DORY. AND I DON'T THINK I'VE EVER EATEN A FISH.
GOOD ON YA! THAT'S INCREDIBLE!
HOW 'BOUT YOU, MATE? WHAT'S ***YOUR*** PROBLEM?
I DON'T HAVE A PROBLEM.
DENIAL.

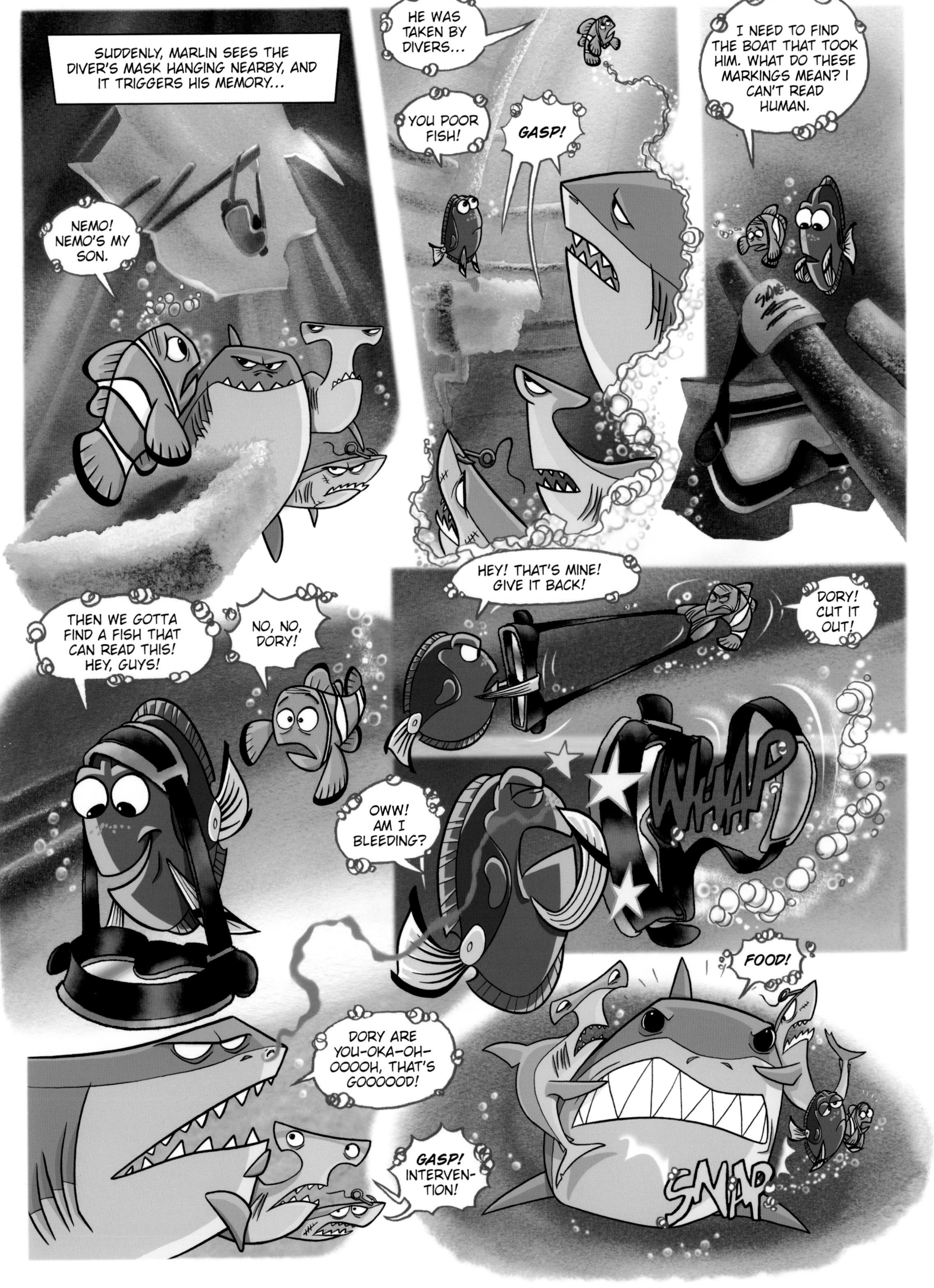
SUDDENLY, MARLIN SEES THE DIVER'S MASK HANGING NEARBY, AND IT TRIGGERS HIS MEMORY...
NEMO! NEMO'S MY SON.
HE WAS TAKEN BY DIVERS...
YOU POOR FISH!
GASP!
I NEED TO FIND THE BOAT THAT TOOK HIM. WHAT DO THESE MARKINGS MEAN? I CAN'T READ HUMAN.
THEN WE GOTTA FIND A FISH THAT CAN READ THIS! HEY, GUYS!
NO, NO, DORY!
HEY! THAT'S MINE! GIVE IT BACK!
DORY! CUT IT OUT!
OWW! AM I BLEEDING?
WHAP
DORY ARE YOU-OKA-OH-OOOOH, THAT'S GOOOOOD!
GASP! INTERVEN-TION!
FOOD!
SNAP

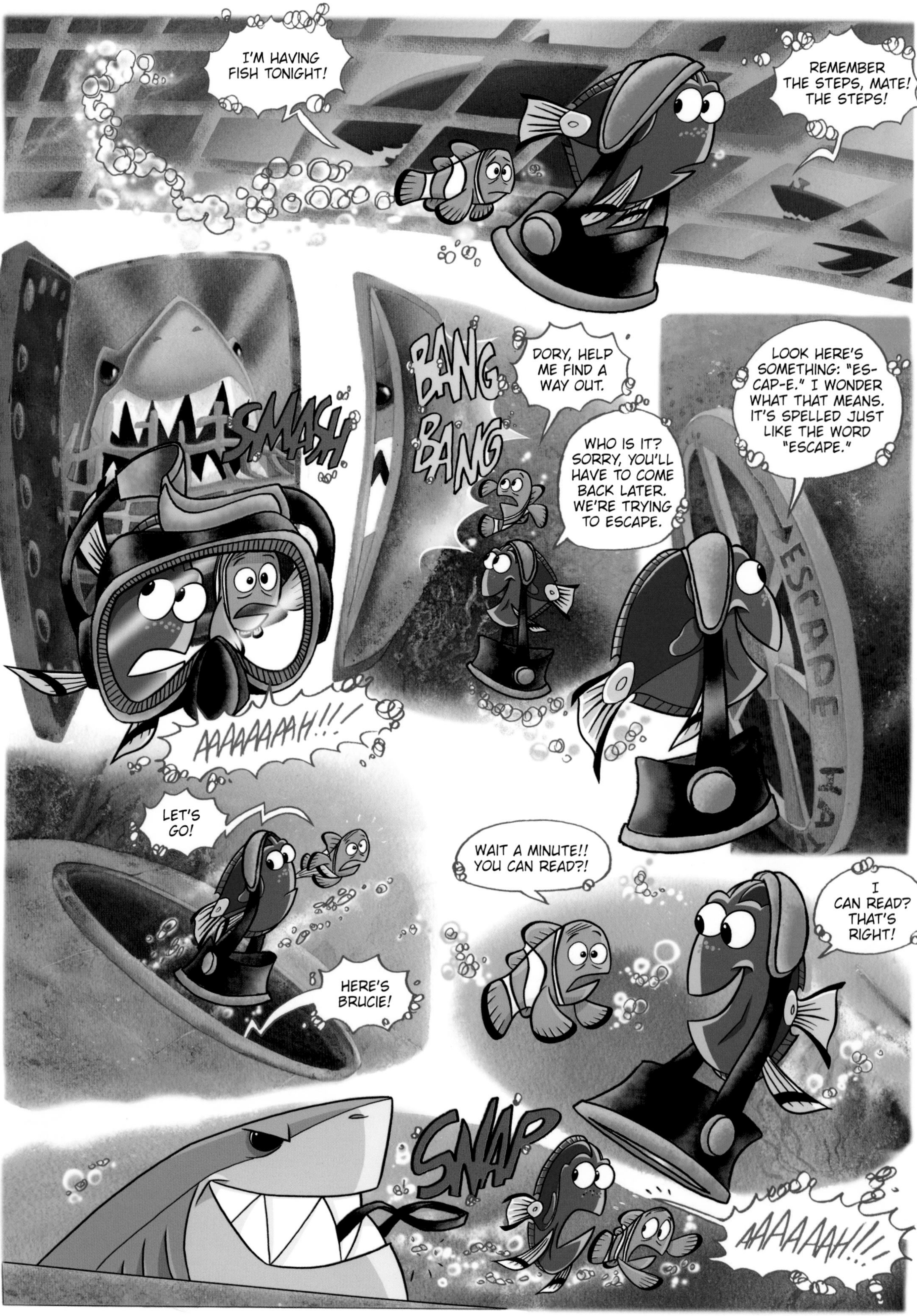
I'M HAVING FISH TONIGHT!
REMEMBER THE STEPS, MATE! THE STEPS!
SMASH
BANG BANG
DORY, HELP ME FIND A WAY OUT.
WHO IS IT? SORRY, YOU'LL HAVE TO COME BACK LATER. WE'RE TRYING TO ESCAPE.
LOOK HERE'S SOMETHING: "ES-CAP-E." I WONDER WHAT THAT MEANS. IT'S SPELLED JUST LIKE THE WORD "ESCAPE."
ESCAPE
AAAAAAAAH!!!
LET'S GO!
HERE'S BRUCIE!
WAIT A MINUTE!! YOU CAN READ?!
I CAN READ? THAT'S RIGHT!
SNAP
AAAAAAH!!!

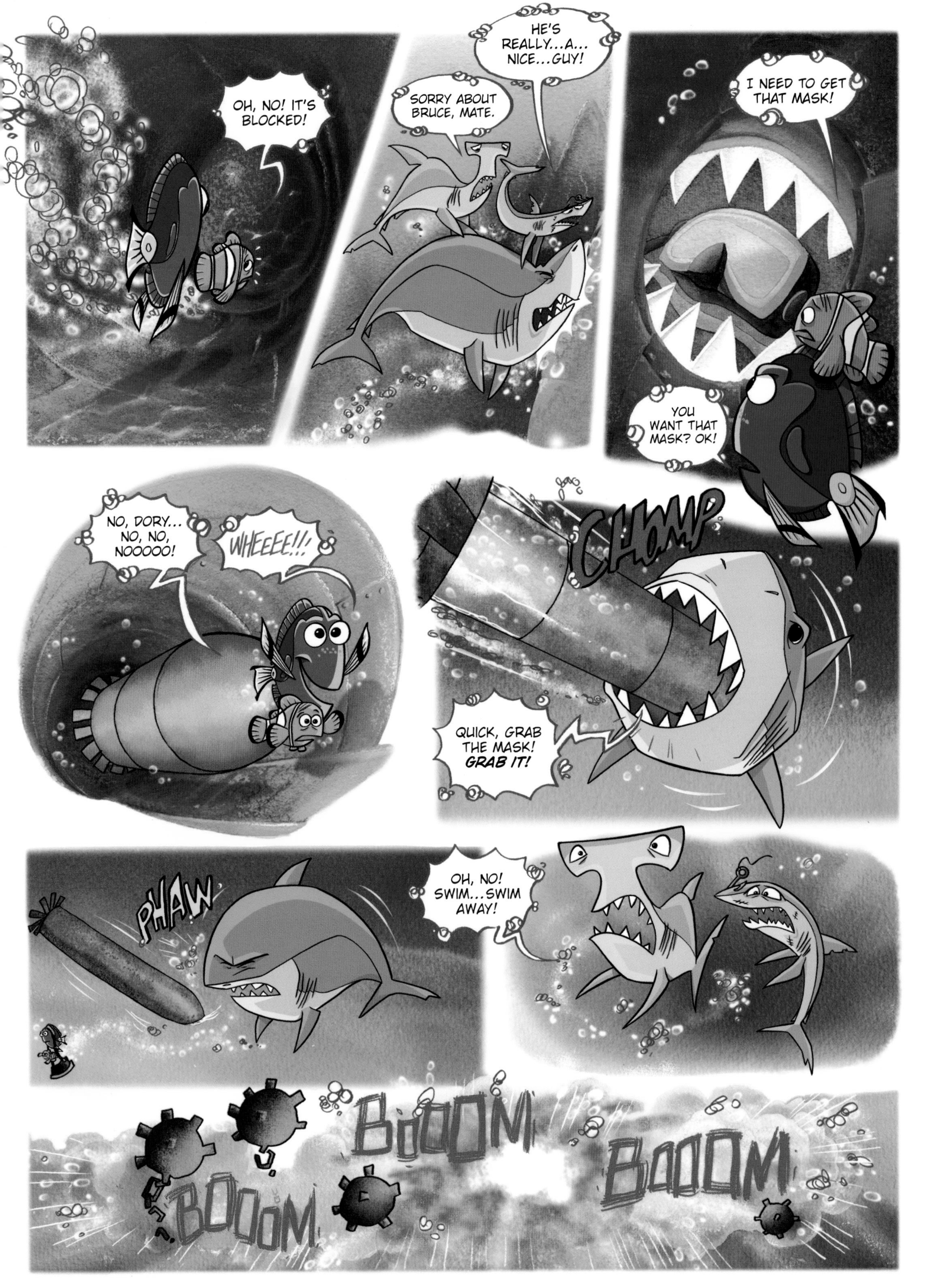
OH, NO! IT'S BLOCKED!
SORRY ABOUT BRUCE, MATE.
HE'S REALLY...A... NICE...GUY!
I NEED TO GET THAT MASK!
YOU WANT THAT MASK? OK!
NO, DORY... NO, NO, NOOOOO!
WHEEEE!!!
CHOMP
QUICK, GRAB THE MASK! GRAB IT!
PHAW
OH, NO! SWIM...SWIM AWAY!
BOOOM
BOOOM
BOOOM

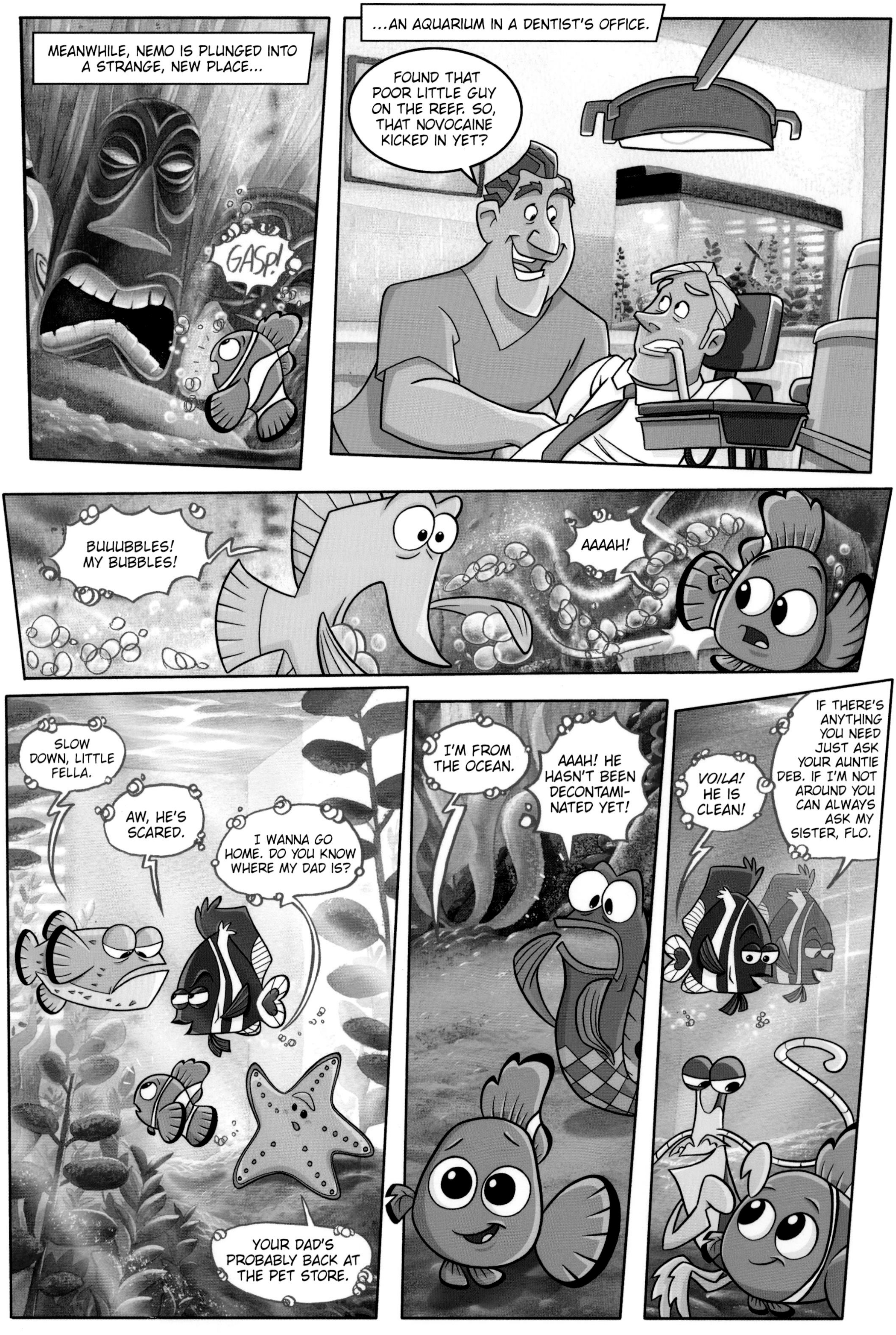
MEANWHILE, NEMO IS PLUNGED INTO A STRANGE, NEW PLACE...
GASP!
...AN AQUARIUM IN A DENTIST'S OFFICE.
FOUND THAT POOR LITTLE GUY ON THE REEF. SO, THAT NOVOCAINE KICKED IN YET?
BUUUBBLES! MY BUBBLES!
AAAAH!
SLOW DOWN, LITTLE FELLA.
AW, HE'S SCARED.
I WANNA GO HOME. DO YOU KNOW WHERE MY DAD IS?
YOUR DAD'S PROBABLY BACK AT THE PET STORE.
I'M FROM THE OCEAN.
AAAH! HE HASN'T BEEN DECONTAMI-NATED YET!
VOILA! HE IS CLEAN!
IF THERE'S ANYTHING YOU NEED JUST ASK YOUR AUNTIE DEB. IF I'M NOT AROUND YOU CAN ALWAYS ASK MY SISTER, FLO.

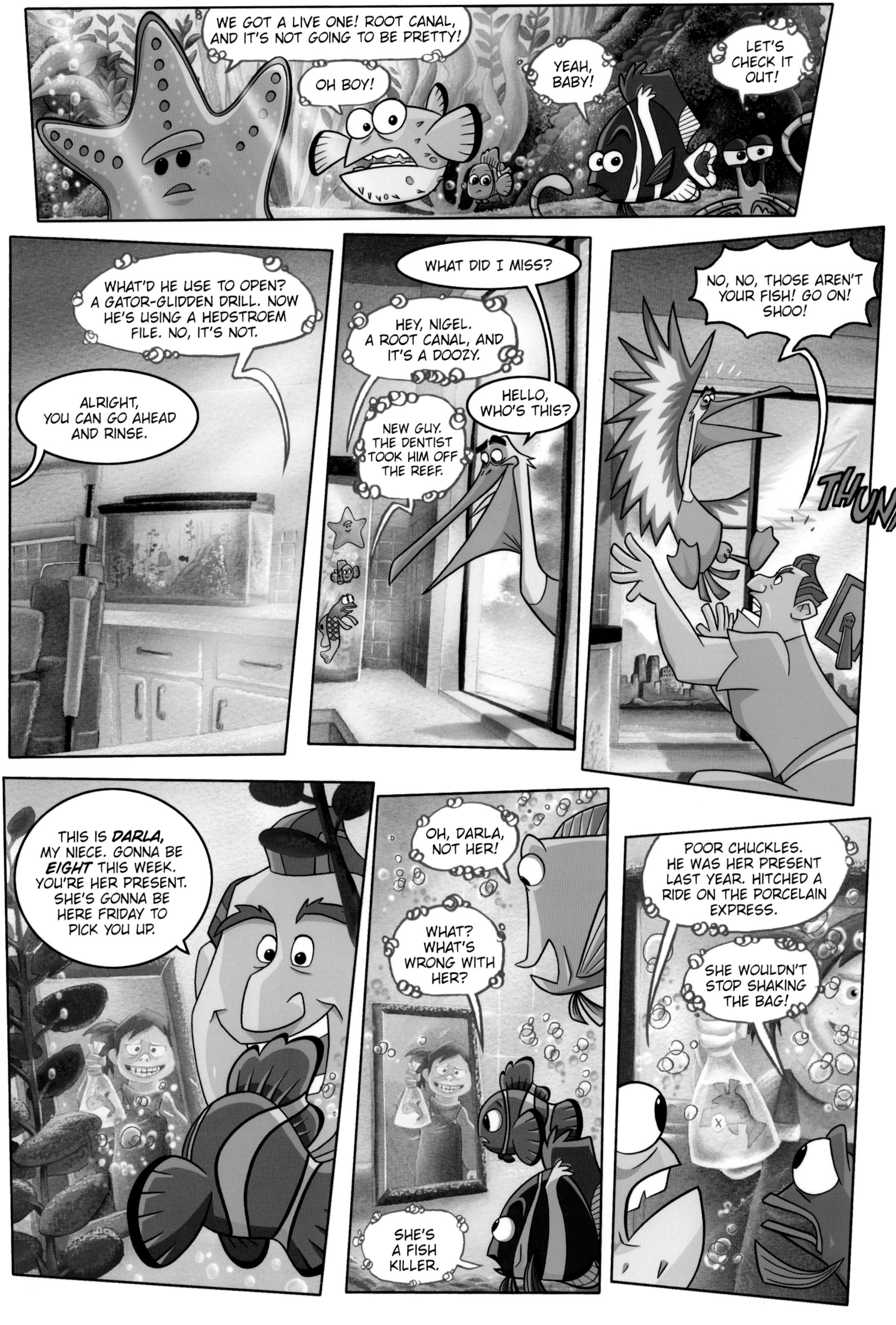

WE GOT A LIVE ONE! ROOT CANAL, AND IT'S NOT GOING TO BE PRETTY!
OH BOY!
YEAH, BABY!
LET'S CHECK IT OUT!
WHAT'D HE USE TO OPEN? A GATOR-GLIDDEN DRILL. NOW HE'S USING A HEDSTROEM FILE. NO, IT'S NOT.
ALRIGHT, YOU CAN GO AHEAD AND RINSE.
WHAT DID I MISS?
HEY, NIGEL. A ROOT CANAL, AND IT'S A DOOZY.
HELLO, WHO'S THIS?
NEW GUY. THE DENTIST TOOK HIM OFF THE REEF.
NO, NO, THOSE AREN'T YOUR FISH! GO ON! SHOO!
THUNK
THIS IS DARLA, MY NIECE. GONNA BE EIGHT THIS WEEK. YOU'RE HER PRESENT. SHE'S GONNA BE HERE FRIDAY TO PICK YOU UP.
OH, DARLA, NOT HER!
WHAT? WHAT'S WRONG WITH HER?
SHE'S A FISH KILLER.
POOR CHUCKLES. HE WAS HER PRESENT LAST YEAR. HITCHED A RIDE ON THE PORCELAIN EXPRESS.
SHE WOULDN'T STOP SHAKING THE BAG!

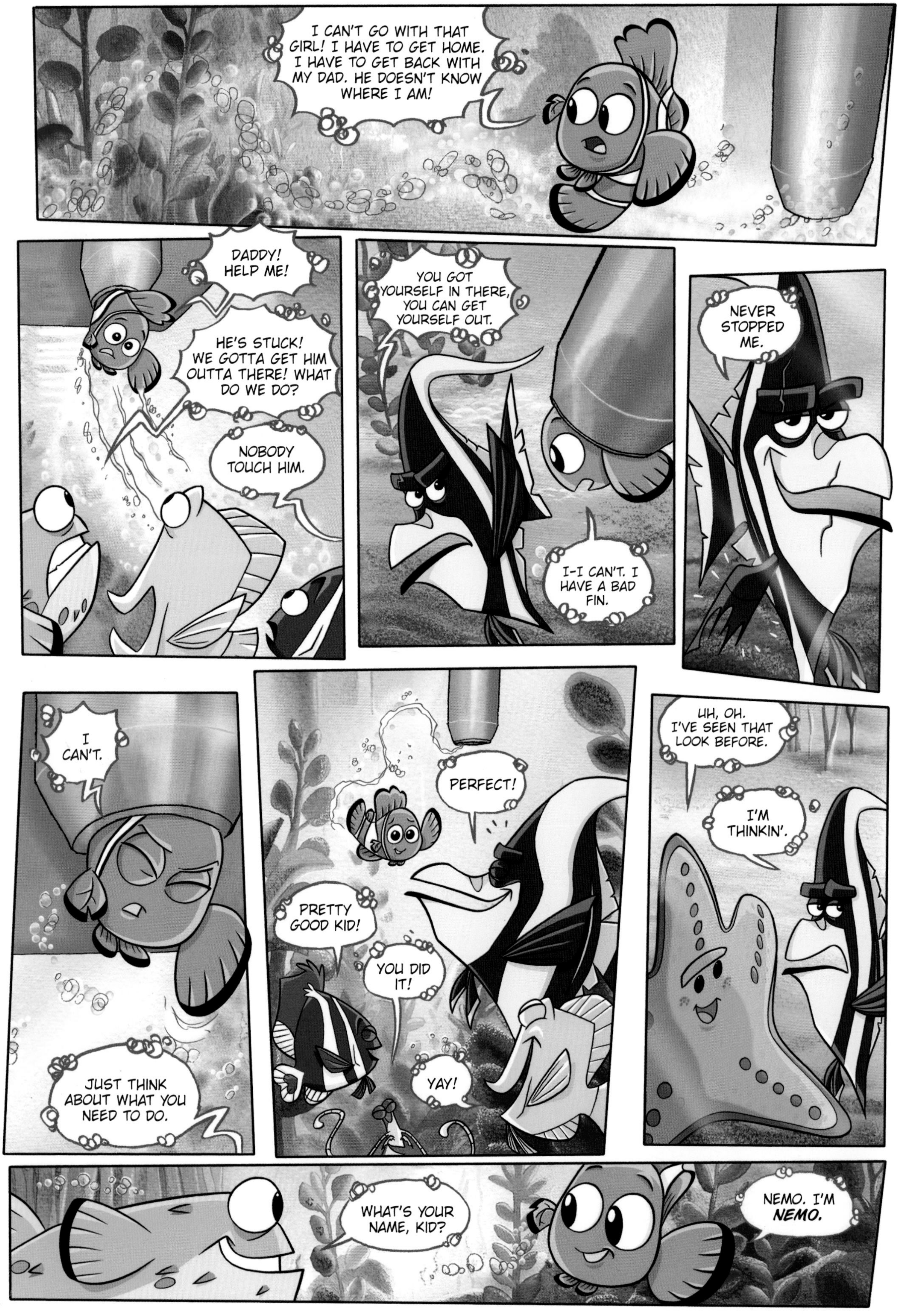
I CAN'T GO WITH THAT GIRL! I HAVE TO GET HOME. I HAVE TO GET BACK WITH MY DAD. HE DOESN'T KNOW WHERE I AM!
DADDY! HELP ME!
HE'S STUCK! WE GOTTA GET HIM OUTTA THERE! WHAT DO WE DO?
NOBODY TOUCH HIM.
YOU GOT YOURSELF IN THERE, YOU CAN GET YOURSELF OUT.
I-I CAN'T. I HAVE A BAD FIN.
NEVER STOPPED ME.
I CAN'T.
JUST THINK ABOUT WHAT YOU NEED TO DO.
PERFECT!
PRETTY GOOD KID!
YOU DID IT!
YAY!
UH, OH. I'VE SEEN THAT LOOK BEFORE.
I'M THINKIN'.
WHAT'S YOUR NAME, KID?
NEMO. I'M *NEMO.*

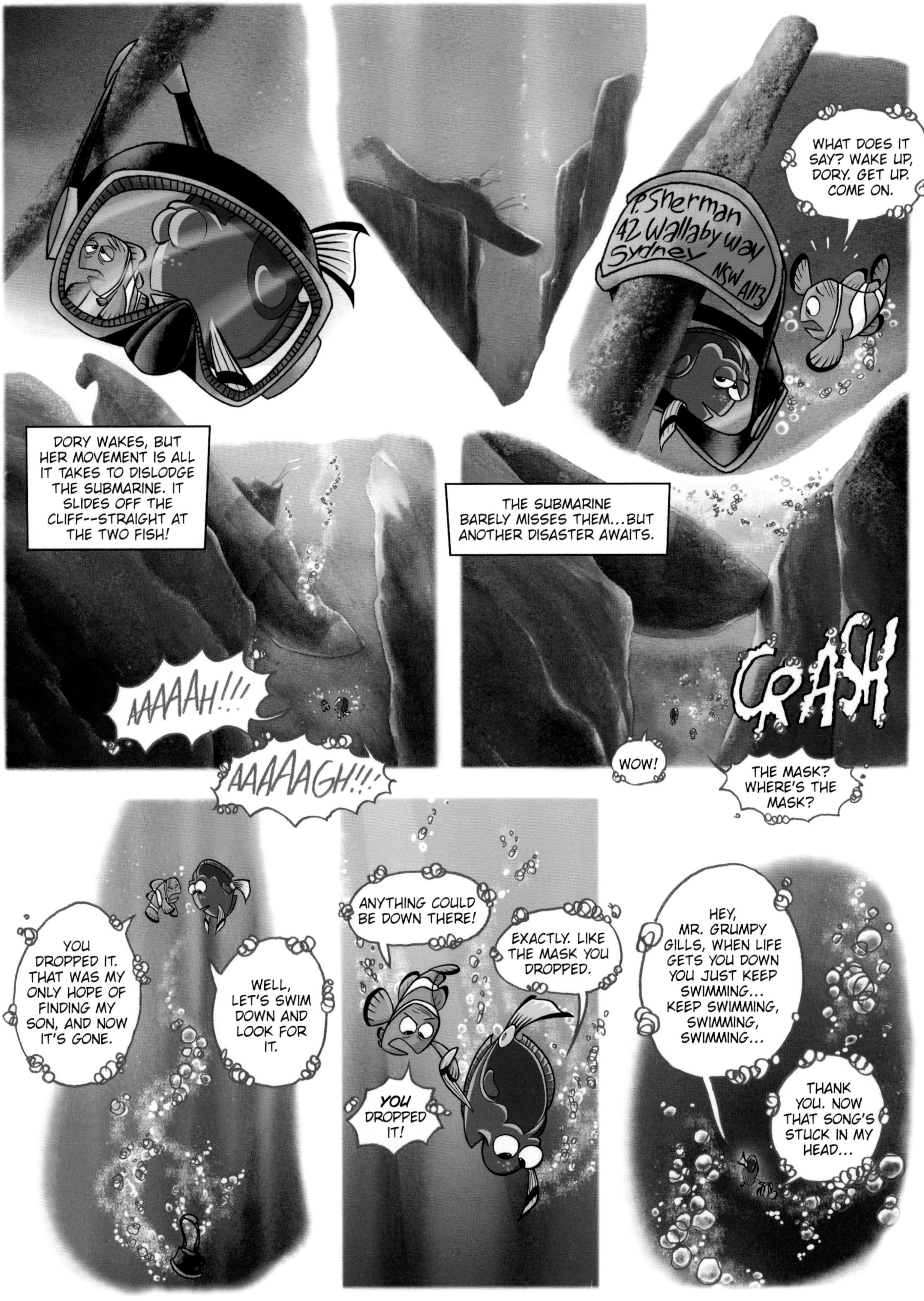
P. Sherman 42 Wallaby way Sydney NSW A113
WHAT DOES IT SAY? WAKE UP, DORY. GET UP. COME ON.
DORY WAKES, BUT HER MOVEMENT IS ALL IT TAKES TO DISLODGE THE SUBMARINE. IT SLIDES OFF THE CLIFF--STRAIGHT AT THE TWO FISH!
AAAAAH!!!
AAAAAGH!!!
THE SUBMARINE BARELY MISSES THEM...BUT ANOTHER DISASTER AWAITS.
CRASH
WOW!
THE MASK? WHERE'S THE MASK?
YOU DROPPED IT. THAT WAS MY ONLY HOPE OF FINDING MY SON, AND NOW IT'S GONE.
WELL, LET'S SWIM DOWN AND LOOK FOR IT.
ANYTHING COULD BE DOWN THERE!
EXACTLY. LIKE THE MASK YOU DROPPED.
YOU DROPPED IT!
HEY, MR. GRUMPY GILLS, WHEN LIFE GETS YOU DOWN YOU JUST KEEP SWIMMING... KEEP SWIMMING, SWIMMING, SWIMMING...
THANK YOU. NOW THAT SONG'S STUCK IN MY HEAD...

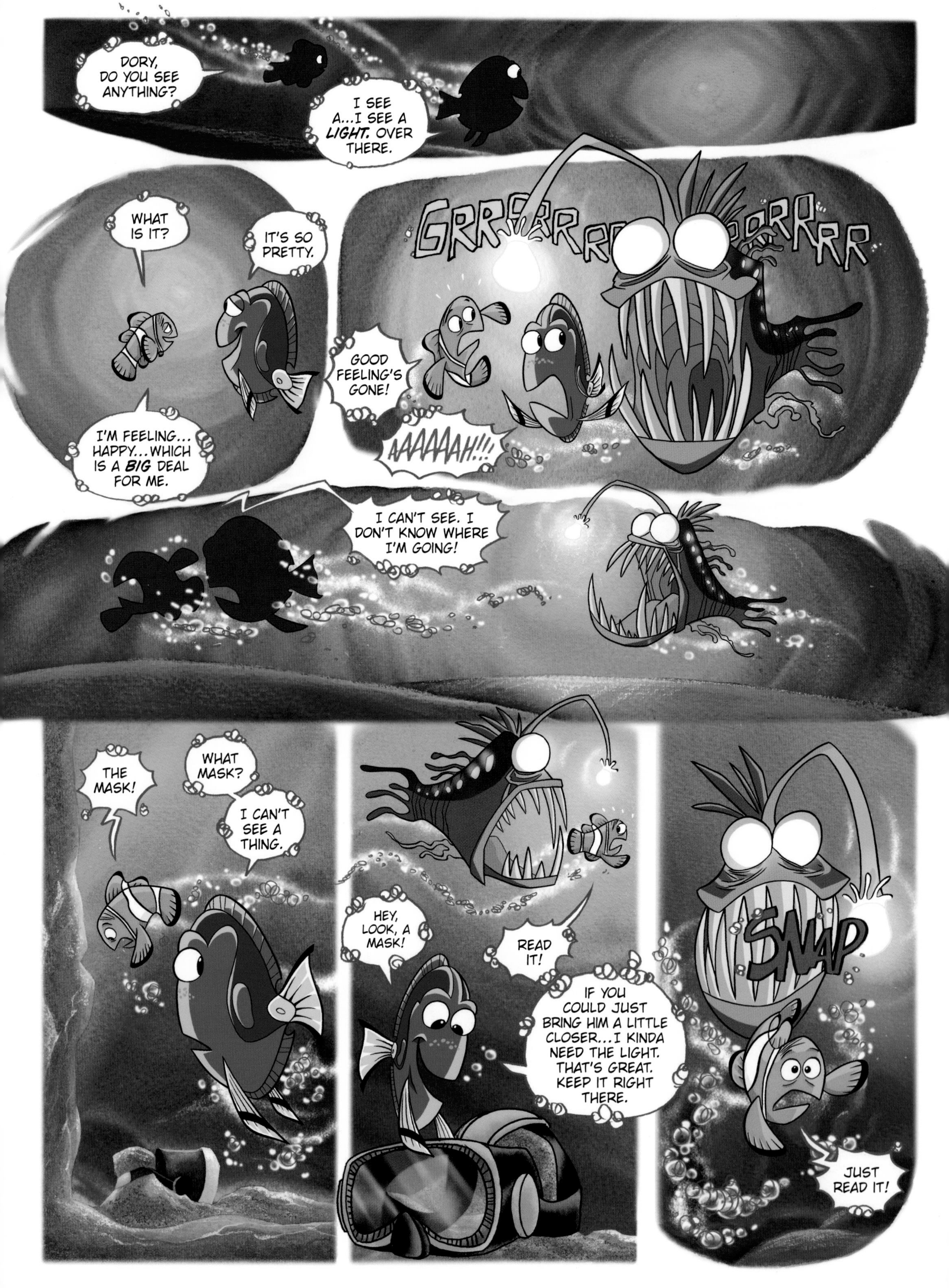
DORY, DO YOU SEE ANYTHING?
I SEE A...I SEE A LIGHT. OVER THERE.
WHAT IS IT?
IT'S SO PRETTY.
I'M FEELING... HAPPY...WHICH IS A BIG DEAL FOR ME.
GRRRRRRRRRRRRRR
GOOD FEELING'S GONE!
AAAAAAH!!!
I CAN'T SEE. I DON'T KNOW WHERE I'M GOING!
THE MASK!
WHAT MASK?
I CAN'T SEE A THING.
HEY, LOOK, A MASK!
READ IT!
IF YOU COULD JUST BRING HIM A LITTLE CLOSER...I KINDA NEED THE LIGHT. THAT'S GREAT. KEEP IT RIGHT THERE.
SNAP
JUST READ IT!

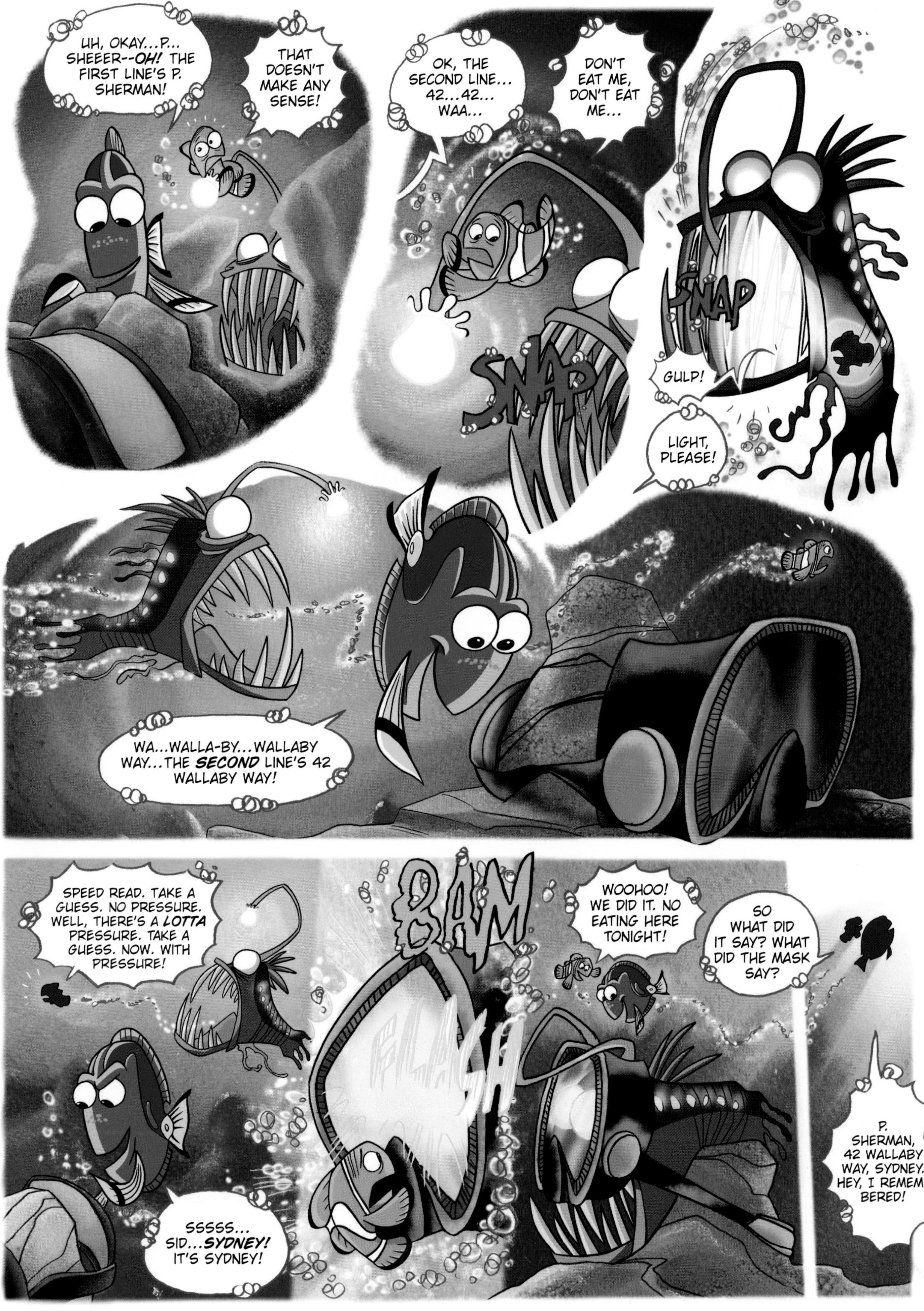
UH, OKAY...P... SHEEER--OH! THE FIRST LINE'S P. SHERMAN!
THAT DOESN'T MAKE ANY SENSE!
OK, THE SECOND LINE... 42...42... WAA...
DON'T EAT ME, DON'T EAT ME...
SNAP
SNAP
GULP!
LIGHT, PLEASE!
WA...WALLA-BY...WALLABY WAY...THE SECOND LINE'S 42 WALLABY WAY!
SPEED READ. TAKE A GUESS. NO PRESSURE. WELL, THERE'S A LOTTA PRESSURE. TAKE A GUESS. NOW. WITH PRESSURE!
SSSSS... SID...SYDNEY! IT'S SYDNEY!
BAM
FLASH
WOOHOO! WE DID IT. NO EATING HERE TONIGHT!
SO WHAT DID IT SAY? WHAT DID THE MASK SAY?
P. SHERMAN, 42 WALLABY WAY, SYDNEY. HEY, I REMEMBERED!

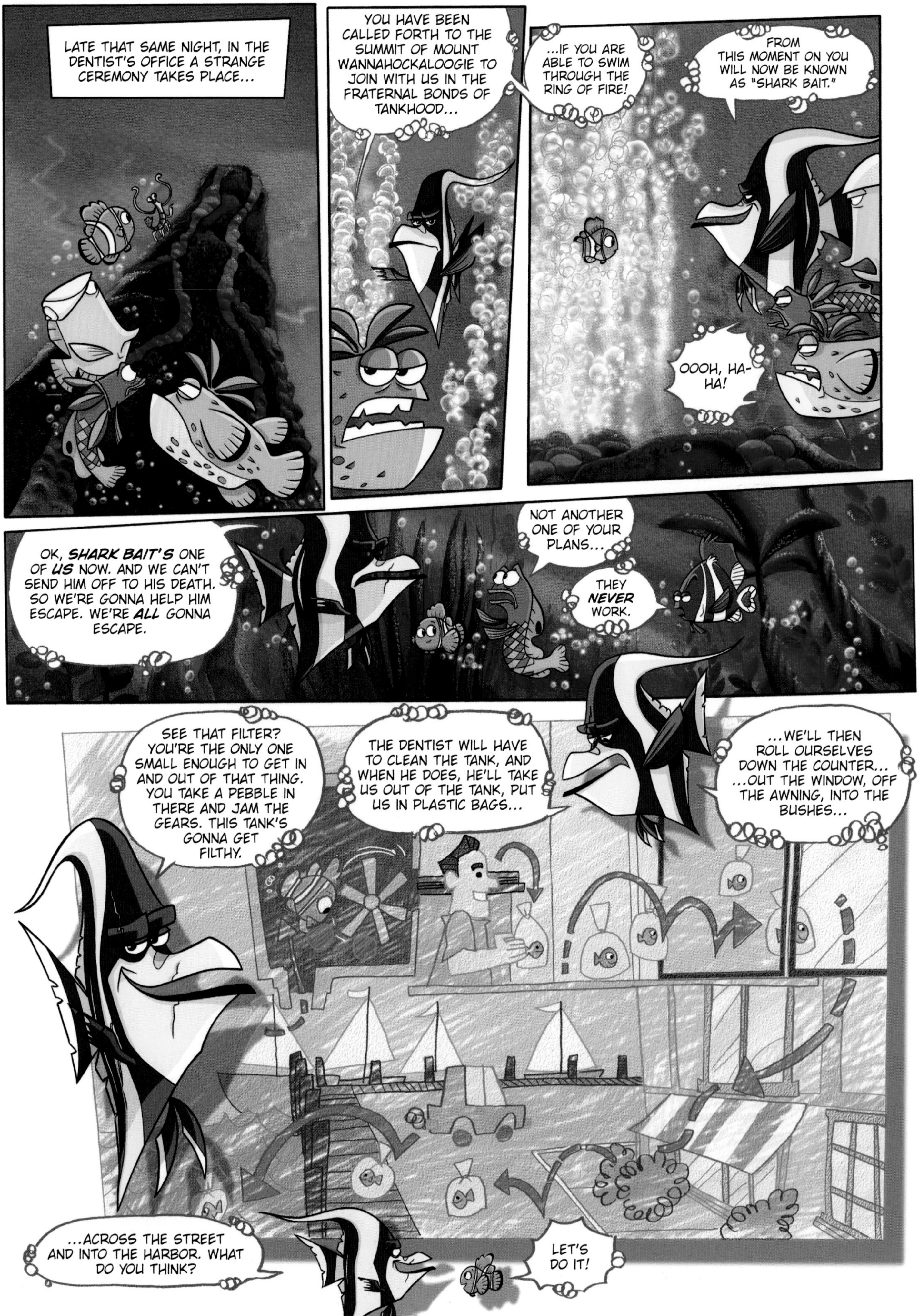
LATE THAT SAME NIGHT, IN THE DENTIST'S OFFICE A STRANGE CEREMONY TAKES PLACE...
YOU HAVE BEEN CALLED FORTH TO THE SUMMIT OF MOUNT WANNAHOCKALOOGIE TO JOIN WITH US IN THE FRATERNAL BONDS OF TANKHOOD...
...IF YOU ARE ABLE TO SWIM THROUGH THE RING OF FIRE!
FROM THIS MOMENT ON YOU WILL NOW BE KNOWN AS "SHARK BAIT."
OOOH, HA-HA!
OK, ***SHARK BAIT'S*** ONE OF ***US*** NOW. AND WE CAN'T SEND HIM OFF TO HIS DEATH. SO WE'RE GONNA HELP HIM ESCAPE. WE'RE ***ALL*** GONNA ESCAPE.
NOT ANOTHER ONE OF YOUR PLANS...
THEY ***NEVER*** WORK.
SEE THAT FILTER? YOU'RE THE ONLY ONE SMALL ENOUGH TO GET IN AND OUT OF THAT THING. YOU TAKE A PEBBLE IN THERE AND JAM THE GEARS. THIS TANK'S GONNA GET FILTHY.
THE DENTIST WILL HAVE TO CLEAN THE TANK, AND WHEN HE DOES, HE'LL TAKE US OUT OF THE TANK, PUT US IN PLASTIC BAGS...
...WE'LL THEN ROLL OURSELVES DOWN THE COUNTER... ...OUT THE WINDOW, OFF THE AWNING, INTO THE BUSHES...
...ACROSS THE STREET AND INTO THE HARBOR. WHAT DO YOU THINK?
LET'S DO IT!

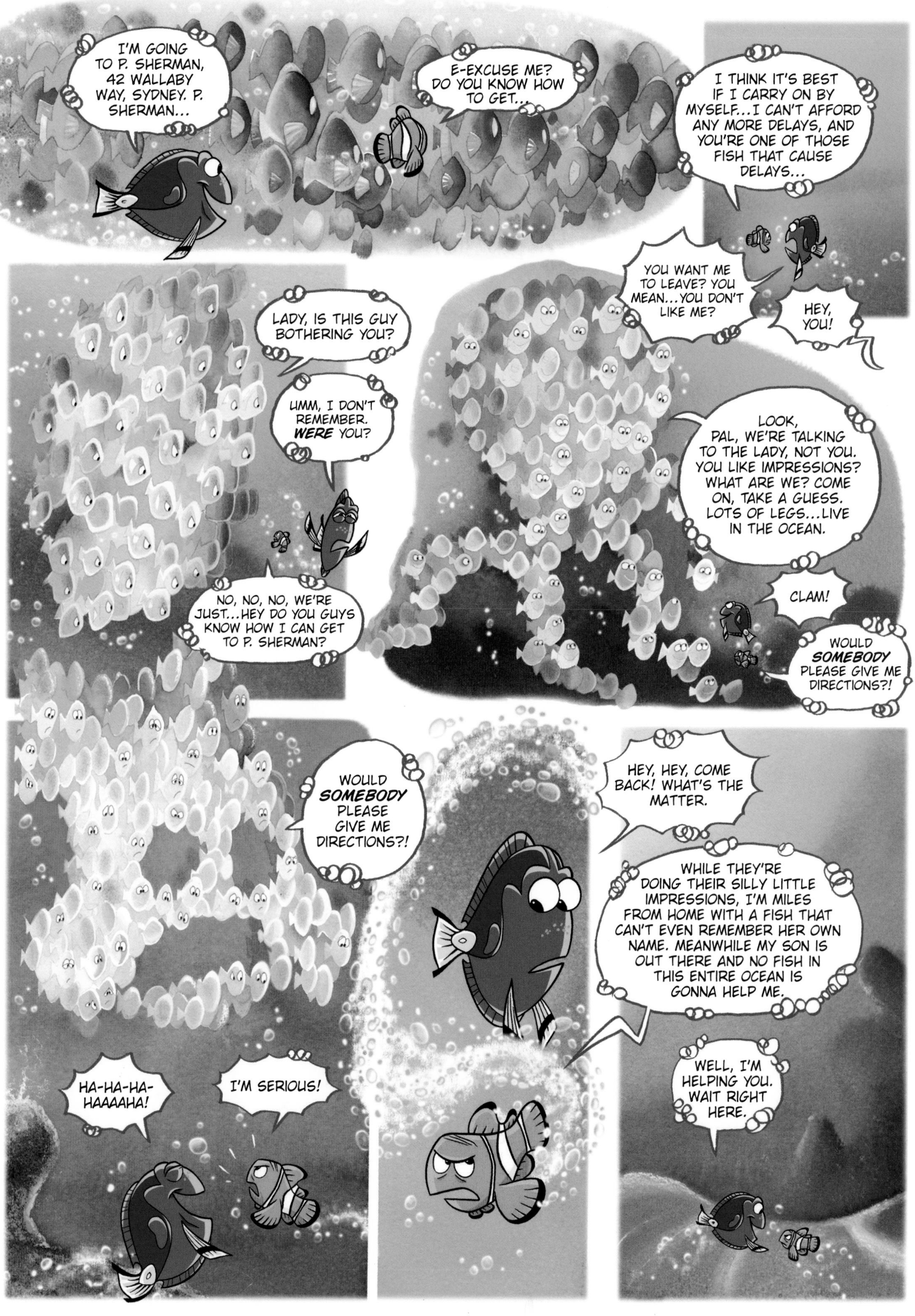

I'M GOING TO P. SHERMAN, 42 WALLABY WAY, SYDNEY. P. SHERMAN...
E-EXCUSE ME? DO YOU KNOW HOW TO GET...
I THINK IT'S BEST IF I CARRY ON BY MYSELF...I CAN'T AFFORD ANY MORE DELAYS, AND YOU'RE ONE OF THOSE FISH THAT CAUSE DELAYS...
YOU WANT ME TO LEAVE? YOU MEAN...YOU DON'T LIKE ME?
HEY, YOU!
LADY, IS THIS GUY BOTHERING YOU?
UMM, I DON'T REMEMBER. *WERE* YOU?
NO, NO, NO, WE'RE JUST...HEY DO YOU GUYS KNOW HOW I CAN GET TO P. SHERMAN?
LOOK, PAL, WE'RE TALKING TO THE LADY, NOT YOU. YOU LIKE IMPRESSIONS? WHAT ARE WE? COME ON, TAKE A GUESS. LOTS OF LEGS...LIVE IN THE OCEAN.
CLAM!
WOULD **SOMEBODY** PLEASE GIVE ME DIRECTIONS?!
WOULD **SOMEBODY** PLEASE GIVE ME DIRECTIONS?!
HA-HA-HA-HAAAAHA!
I'M SERIOUS!
HEY, HEY, COME BACK! WHAT'S THE MATTER.
WHILE THEY'RE DOING THEIR SILLY LITTLE IMPRESSIONS, I'M MILES FROM HOME WITH A FISH THAT CAN'T EVEN REMEMBER HER OWN NAME. MEANWHILE MY SON IS OUT THERE AND NO FISH IN THIS ENTIRE OCEAN IS GONNA HELP ME.
WELL, I'M HELPING YOU. WAIT RIGHT HERE.

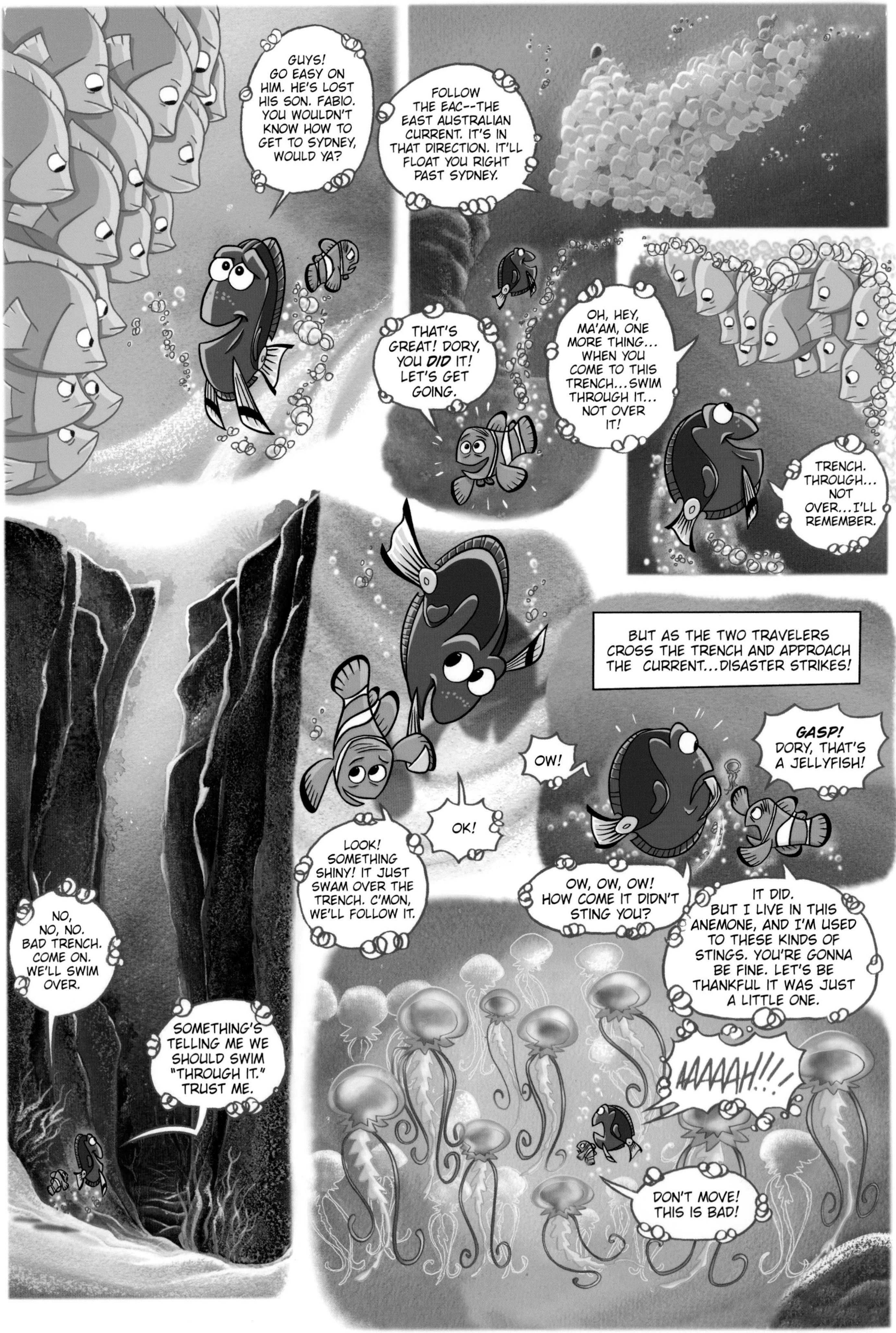
GUYS! GO EASY ON HIM. HE'S LOST HIS SON. FABIO. YOU WOULDN'T KNOW HOW TO GET TO SYDNEY, WOULD YA?
FOLLOW THE EAC--THE EAST AUSTRALIAN CURRENT. IT'S IN THAT DIRECTION. IT'LL FLOAT YOU RIGHT PAST SYDNEY.
THAT'S GREAT! DORY, YOU DID IT! LET'S GET GOING.
OH, HEY, MA'AM, ONE MORE THING... WHEN YOU COME TO THIS TRENCH...SWIM THROUGH IT... NOT OVER IT!
TRENCH. THROUGH... NOT OVER...I'LL REMEMBER.
NO, NO, NO. BAD TRENCH. COME ON. WE'LL SWIM OVER.
SOMETHING'S TELLING ME WE SHOULD SWIM "THROUGH IT." TRUST ME.
LOOK! SOMETHING SHINY! IT JUST SWAM OVER THE TRENCH. C'MON, WE'LL FOLLOW IT.
OK!
BUT AS THE TWO TRAVELERS CROSS THE TRENCH AND APPROACH THE CURRENT...DISASTER STRIKES!
OW!
GASP! DORY, THAT'S A JELLYFISH!
OW, OW, OW! HOW COME IT DIDN'T STING YOU?
IT DID. BUT I LIVE IN THIS ANEMONE, AND I'M USED TO THESE KINDS OF STINGS. YOU'RE GONNA BE FINE. LET'S BE THANKFUL IT WAS JUST A LITTLE ONE.
AAAAAH!!!
DON'T MOVE! THIS IS BAD!

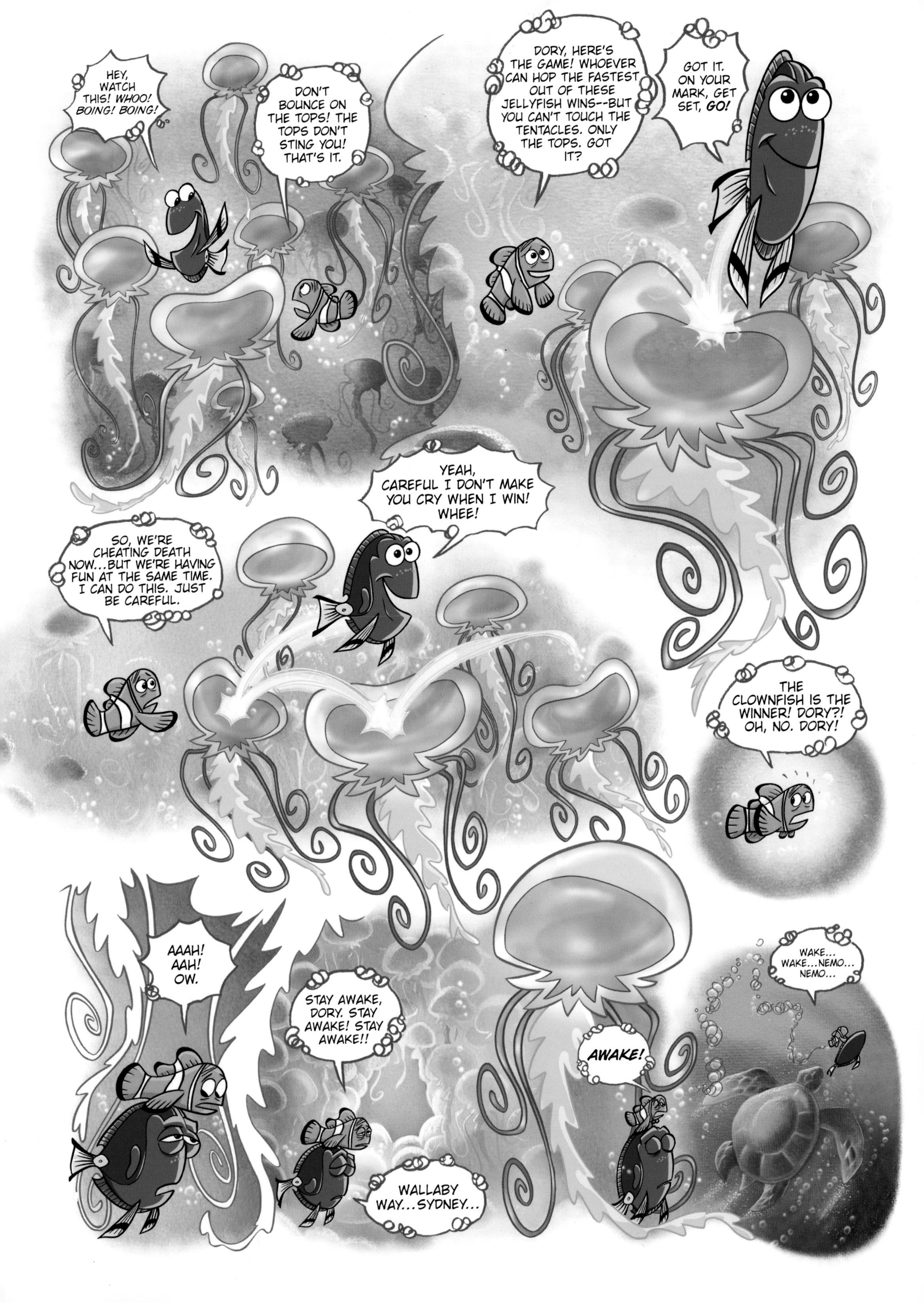

HEY, WATCH THIS! WHOO! BOING! BOING!
DON'T BOUNCE ON THE TOPS! THE TOPS DON'T STING YOU! THAT'S IT.
DORY, HERE'S THE GAME! WHOEVER CAN HOP THE FASTEST OUT OF THESE JELLYFISH WINS--BUT YOU CAN'T TOUCH THE TENTACLES. ONLY THE TOPS. GOT IT?
GOT IT. ON YOUR MARK, GET SET, GO!
YEAH, CAREFUL I DON'T MAKE YOU CRY WHEN I WIN! WHEE!
SO, WE'RE CHEATING DEATH NOW...BUT WE'RE HAVING FUN AT THE SAME TIME. I CAN DO THIS. JUST BE CAREFUL.
THE CLOWNFISH IS THE WINNER! DORY?! OH, NO. DORY!
AAAH! AAH! OW.
STAY AWAKE, DORY. STAY AWAKE! STAY AWAKE!!
WALLABY WAY...SYDNEY...
AWAKE!
WAKE... WAKE...NEMO... NEMO...

MEANWHILE, IN THE AQUARIUM, GILL TEACHES NEMO TO SWIM BETTER...

YOU'RE LOOKIN' AT MY SCARS, AREN'T YOU? THIS ONE HAPPENED WHEN I LANDED ON DENTAL TOOLS. I WAS AIMING FOR THE TOILET.

THE TOILET?

ALL DRAINS LEAD TO THE OCEAN, KID.

YOU MISS YOUR DAD, DON'T YOU? YOU'RE LUCKY TO HAVE SOMEONE OUT THERE WHO'S LOOKIN' FOR YOU.

HE'S NOT LOOKING FOR ME. HE'S SCARED OF THE OCEAN.

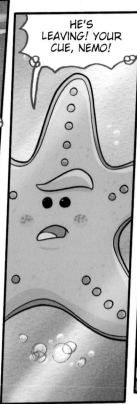

HE'S LEAVING! YOUR CUE, NEMO!

THERE'S A GAP ABOVE THE BIG WATER WHEEL JUST BIG ENOUGH FOR YOU TO LEAP THROUGH. THEN, SWIM TO THE BOTTOM OF THE CHAMBER.

NICELY DONE. HERE COMES THE PEBBLE.

WEDGE THAT PEBBLE UP AGAINST THE ROD TO STOP IT TURNING.

GILL, THIS ISN'T A GOOD IDEA. HE'S JUST A KID.

NEMO SUCCEEDS! BUT AS HE SWIMS BACK UP THE TUBE, THE PEBBLE SLIPS OUT!

GILL!

GET HIM OUTTA THERE!

WHAT DO WE DO? WHAT DO WE DO?

COME ON, SHARK BAIT! GRAB THIS!

PULL!

GILL, DON'T MAKE HIM GO BACK IN THERE.

NO. WE'RE DONE.

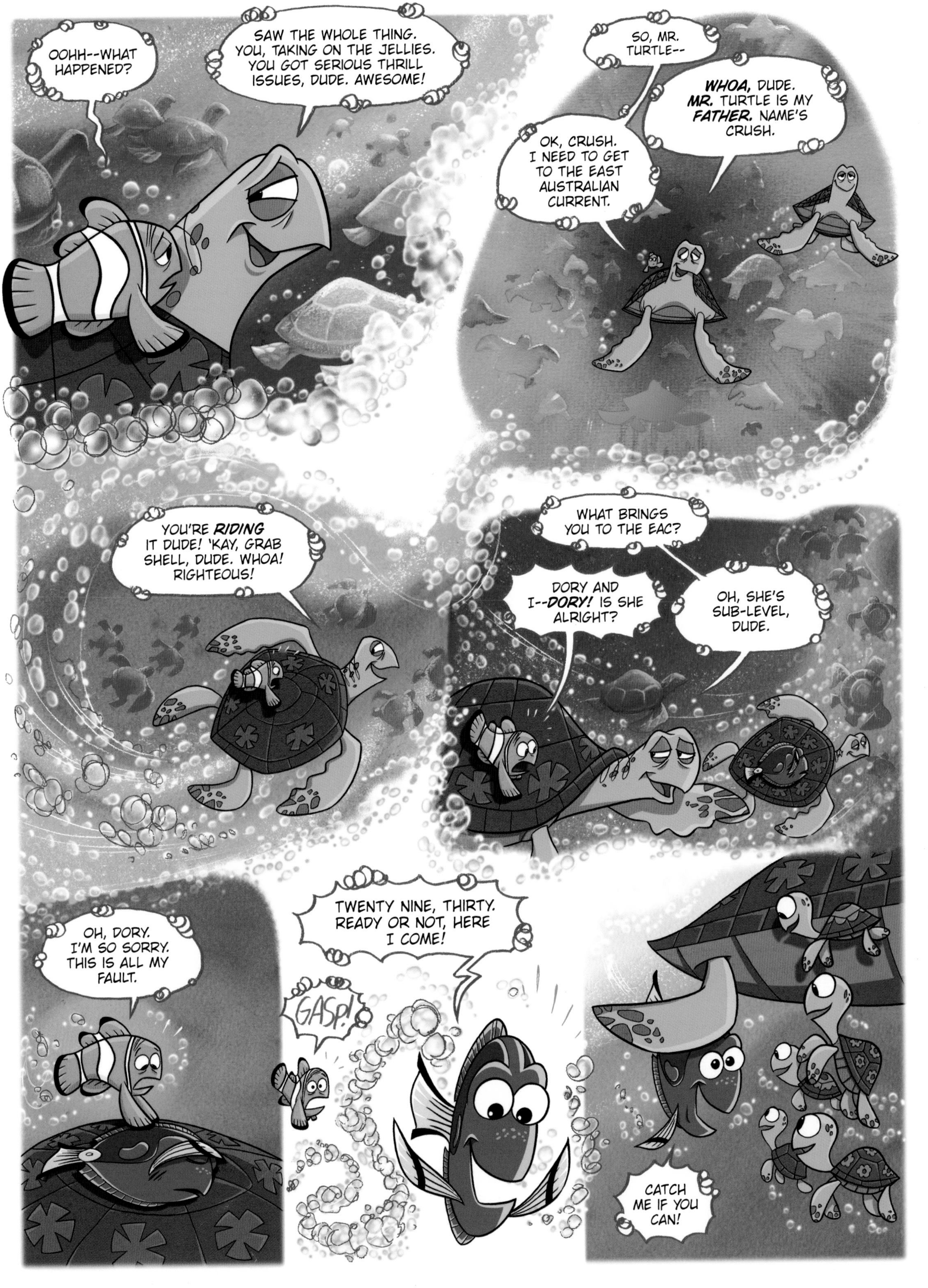
OOHH--WHAT HAPPENED?
SAW THE WHOLE THING. YOU, TAKING ON THE JELLIES. YOU GOT SERIOUS THRILL ISSUES, DUDE. AWESOME!
SO, MR. TURTLE--
WHOA, DUDE. MR. TURTLE IS MY FATHER. NAME'S CRUSH.
OK, CRUSH. I NEED TO GET TO THE EAST AUSTRALIAN CURRENT.
YOU'RE RIDING IT DUDE! 'KAY, GRAB SHELL, DUDE. WHOA! RIGHTEOUS!
WHAT BRINGS YOU TO THE EAC?
DORY AND I--DORY! IS SHE ALRIGHT?
OH, SHE'S SUB-LEVEL, DUDE.
OH, DORY. I'M SO SORRY. THIS IS ALL MY FAULT.
TWENTY NINE, THIRTY. READY OR NOT, HERE I COME!
GASP!
CATCH ME IF YOU CAN!

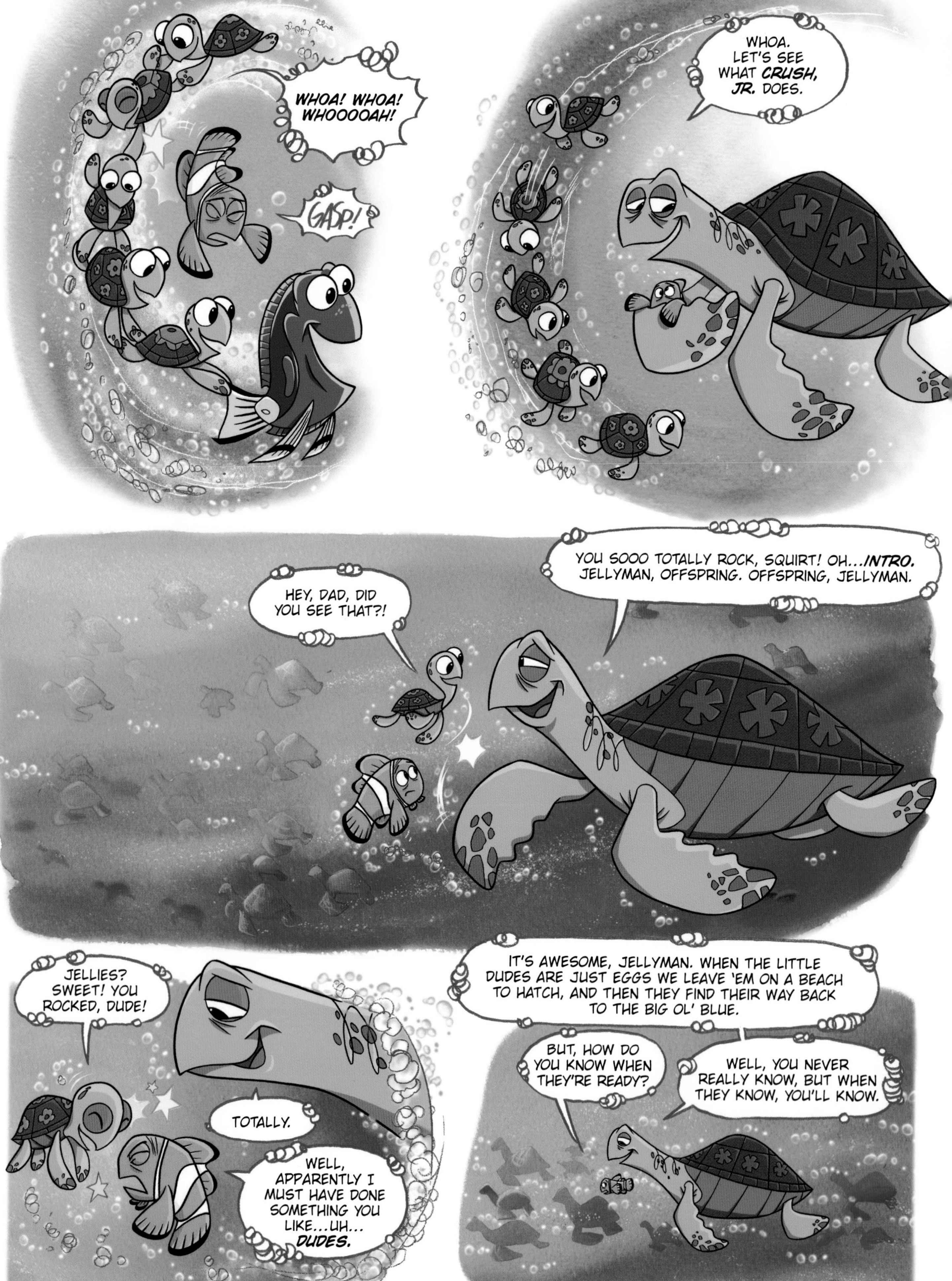
WHOA! WHOA! WHOOOOAH!
GASP!
WHOA. LET'S SEE WHAT CRUSH, JR. DOES.
HEY, DAD, DID YOU SEE THAT?!
YOU SOOO TOTALLY ROCK, SQUIRT! OH...INTRO. JELLYMAN, OFFSPRING. OFFSPRING, JELLYMAN.
JELLIES? SWEET! YOU ROCKED, DUDE!
TOTALLY.
WELL, APPARENTLY I MUST HAVE DONE SOMETHING YOU LIKE...UH... DUDES.
IT'S AWESOME, JELLYMAN. WHEN THE LITTLE DUDES ARE JUST EGGS WE LEAVE 'EM ON A BEACH TO HATCH, AND THEN THEY FIND THEIR WAY BACK TO THE BIG OL' BLUE.
BUT, HOW DO YOU KNOW WHEN THEY'RE READY?
WELL, YOU NEVER REALLY KNOW, BUT WHEN THEY KNOW, YOU'LL KNOW.

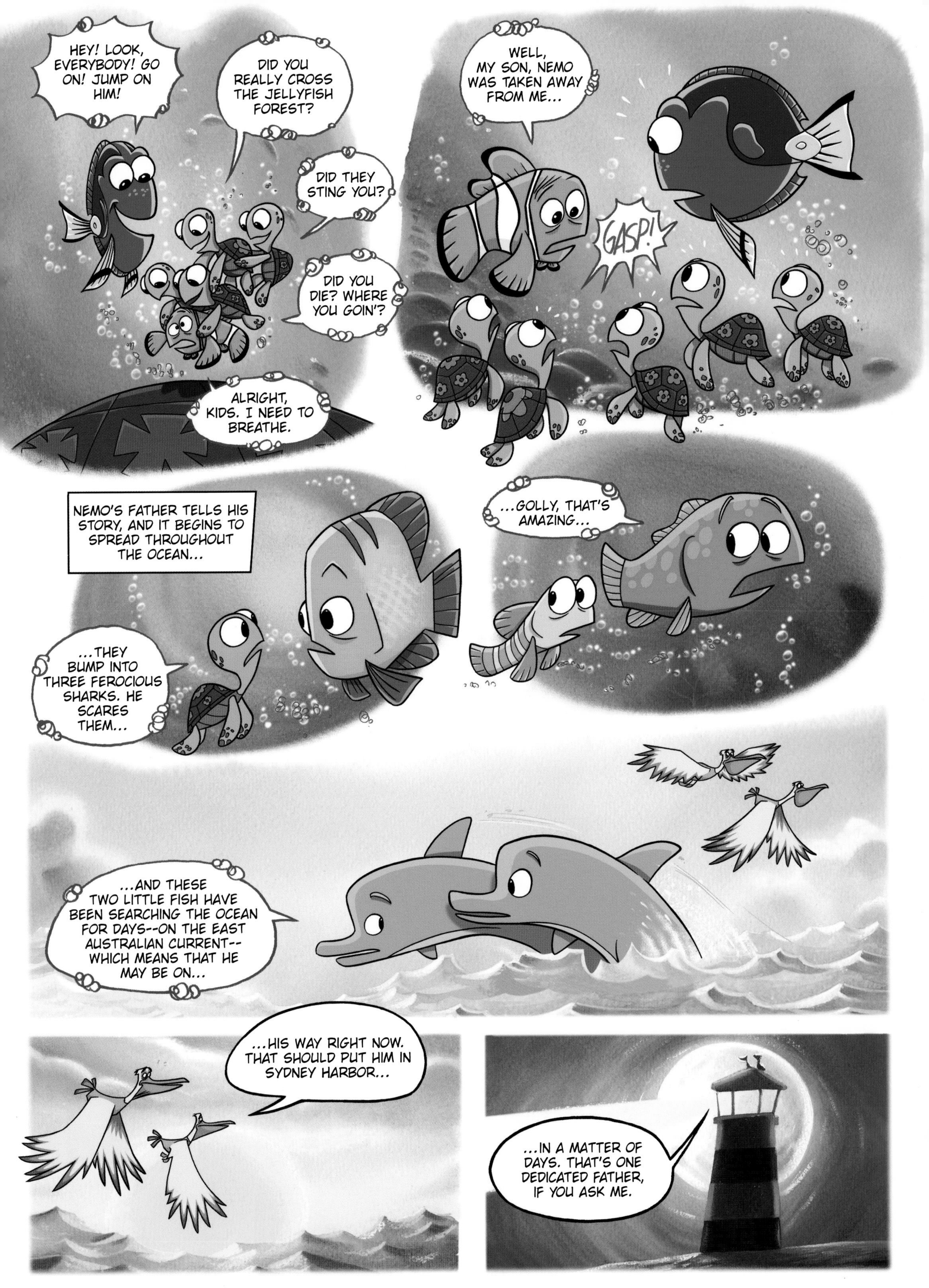
HEY! LOOK, EVERYBODY! GO ON! JUMP ON HIM!
DID YOU REALLY CROSS THE JELLYFISH FOREST?
DID THEY STING YOU?
DID YOU DIE? WHERE YOU GOIN'?
ALRIGHT, KIDS. I NEED TO BREATHE.
WELL, MY SON, NEMO WAS TAKEN AWAY FROM ME...
GASP!
NEMO'S FATHER TELLS HIS STORY, AND IT BEGINS TO SPREAD THROUGHOUT THE OCEAN...
...THEY BUMP INTO THREE FEROCIOUS SHARKS. HE SCARES THEM...
...GOLLY, THAT'S AMAZING...
...AND THESE TWO LITTLE FISH HAVE BEEN SEARCHING THE OCEAN FOR DAYS--ON THE EAST AUSTRALIAN CURRENT--WHICH MEANS THAT HE MAY BE ON...
...HIS WAY RIGHT NOW. THAT SHOULD PUT HIM IN SYDNEY HARBOR...
...IN A MATTER OF DAYS. THAT'S ONE DEDICATED FATHER, IF YOU ASK ME.

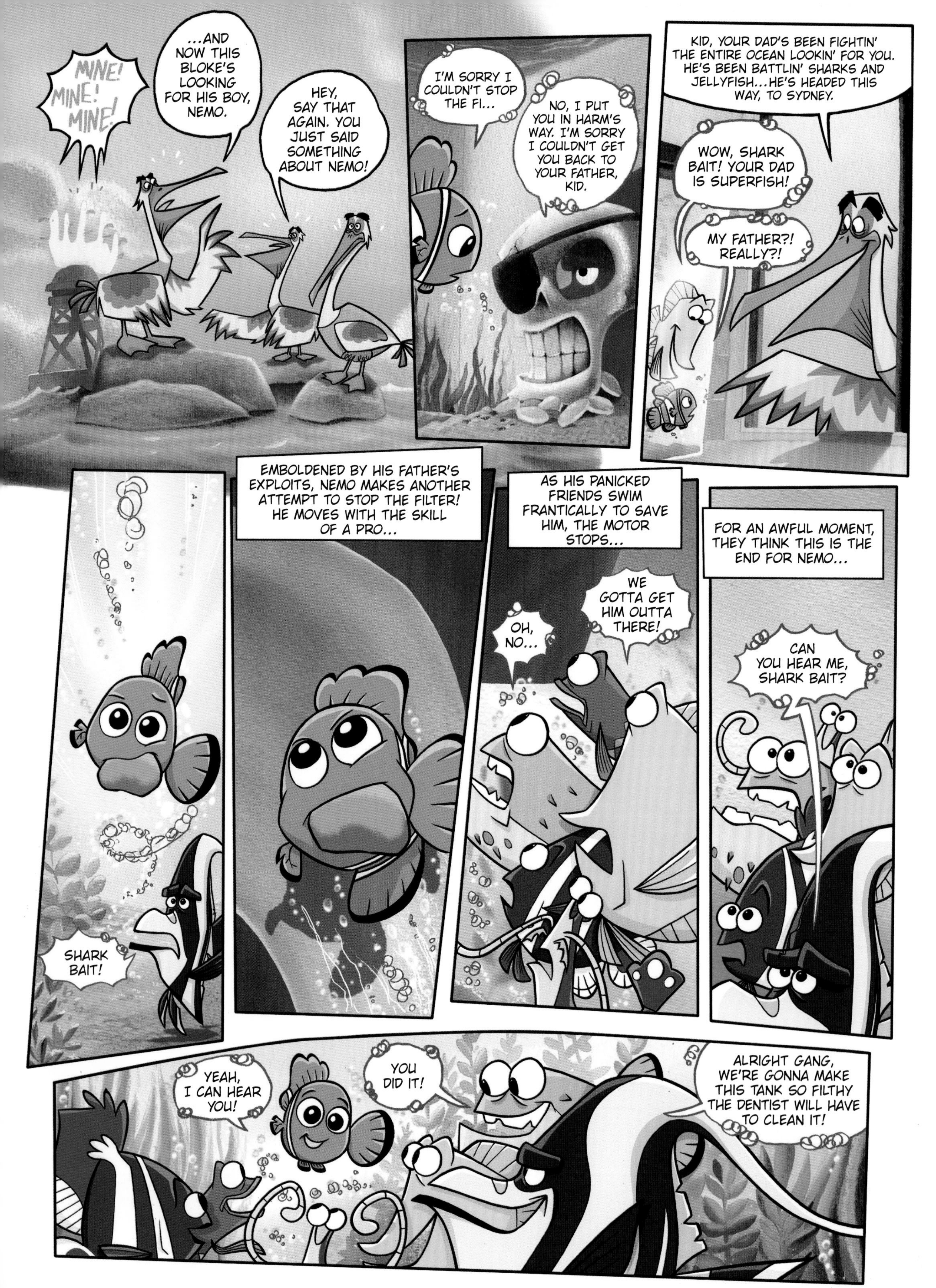
MINE! MINE! MINE!
...AND NOW THIS BLOKE'S LOOKING FOR HIS BOY, NEMO.
HEY, SAY THAT AGAIN. YOU JUST SAID SOMETHING ABOUT NEMO!
I'M SORRY I COULDN'T STOP THE FI...
NO, I PUT YOU IN HARM'S WAY. I'M SORRY I COULDN'T GET YOU BACK TO YOUR FATHER, KID.
KID, YOUR DAD'S BEEN FIGHTIN' THE ENTIRE OCEAN LOOKIN' FOR YOU. HE'S BEEN BATTLIN' SHARKS AND JELLYFISH...HE'S HEADED THIS WAY, TO SYDNEY.
WOW, SHARK BAIT! YOUR DAD IS SUPERFISH!
MY FATHER?! REALLY?!
SHARK BAIT!
EMBOLDENED BY HIS FATHER'S EXPLOITS, NEMO MAKES ANOTHER ATTEMPT TO STOP THE FILTER! HE MOVES WITH THE SKILL OF A PRO...
AS HIS PANICKED FRIENDS SWIM FRANTICALLY TO SAVE HIM, THE MOTOR STOPS...
OH, NO...
WE GOTTA GET HIM OUTTA THERE!
FOR AN AWFUL MOMENT, THEY THINK THIS IS THE END FOR NEMO...
CAN YOU HEAR ME, SHARK BAIT?
YEAH, I CAN HEAR YOU!
YOU DID IT!
ALRIGHT GANG, WE'RE GONNA MAKE THIS TANK SO FILTHY THE DENTIST WILL HAVE TO CLEAN IT!

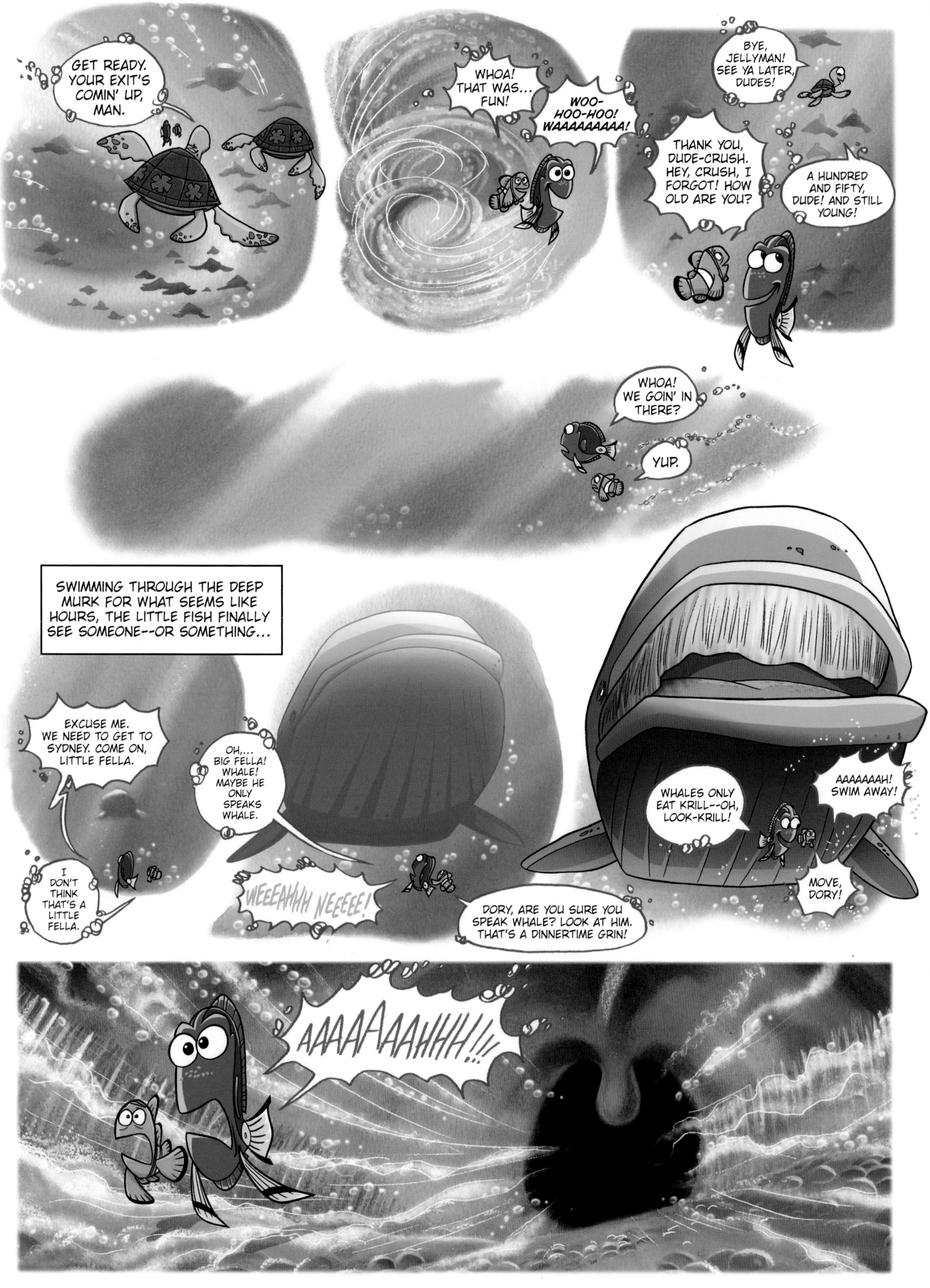
GET READY. YOUR EXIT'S COMIN' UP, MAN.
WHOA! THAT WAS... FUN!
WOO-HOO-HOO! WAAAAAAAAA!
BYE, JELLYMAN! SEE YA LATER, DUDES!
THANK YOU, DUDE-CRUSH. HEY, CRUSH, I FORGOT! HOW OLD ARE YOU?
A HUNDRED AND FIFTY, DUDE! AND STILL YOUNG!
WHOA! WE GOIN' IN THERE?
YUP.
SWIMMING THROUGH THE DEEP MURK FOR WHAT SEEMS LIKE HOURS, THE LITTLE FISH FINALLY SEE SOMEONE--OR SOMETHING...
EXCUSE ME. WE NEED TO GET TO SYDNEY. COME ON, LITTLE FELLA.
I DON'T THINK THAT'S A LITTLE FELLA.
OH,... BIG FELLA! WHALE! MAYBE HE ONLY SPEAKS WHALE.
WEEEAHHH NEEEEE!
DORY, ARE YOU SURE YOU SPEAK WHALE? LOOK AT HIM. THAT'S A DINNERTIME GRIN!
WHALES ONLY EAT KRILL--OH, LOOK-KRILL!
AAAAAAAH! SWIM AWAY!
MOVE, DORY!
AAAAAAAHHH!!!

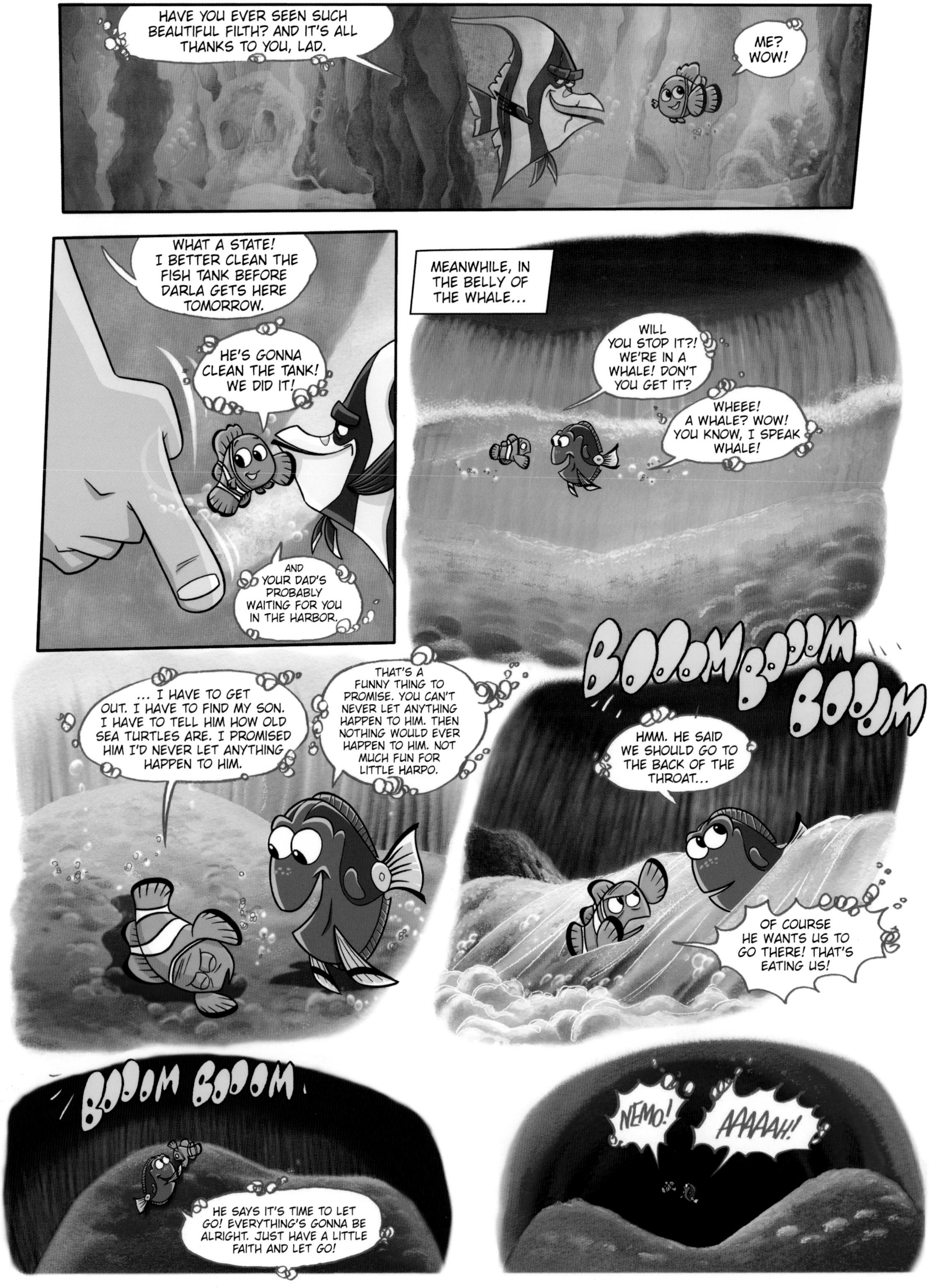
HAVE YOU EVER SEEN SUCH BEAUTIFUL FILTH? AND IT'S ALL THANKS TO YOU, LAD.
ME? WOW!
WHAT A STATE! I BETTER CLEAN THE FISH TANK BEFORE DARLA GETS HERE TOMORROW.
HE'S GONNA CLEAN THE TANK! WE DID IT!
AND YOUR DAD'S PROBABLY WAITING FOR YOU IN THE HARBOR.
MEANWHILE, IN THE BELLY OF THE WHALE...
WILL YOU STOP IT?! WE'RE IN A WHALE! DON'T YOU GET IT?
WHEEE! A WHALE? WOW! YOU KNOW, I SPEAK WHALE!
... I HAVE TO GET OUT. I HAVE TO FIND MY SON. I HAVE TO TELL HIM HOW OLD SEA TURTLES ARE. I PROMISED HIM I'D NEVER LET ANYTHING HAPPEN TO HIM.
THAT'S A FUNNY THING TO PROMISE. YOU CAN'T NEVER LET ANYTHING HAPPEN TO HIM. THEN NOTHING WOULD EVER HAPPEN TO HIM. NOT MUCH FUN FOR LITTLE HARPO.
BOOOM BOOOM BOOOM
HMM. HE SAID WE SHOULD GO TO THE BACK OF THE THROAT...
OF COURSE HE WANTS US TO GO THERE! THAT'S EATING US!
BOOOM BOOOM
HE SAYS IT'S TIME TO LET GO! EVERYTHING'S GONNA BE ALRIGHT. JUST HAVE A LITTLE FAITH AND LET GO!
NEMO!
AAAAAH!

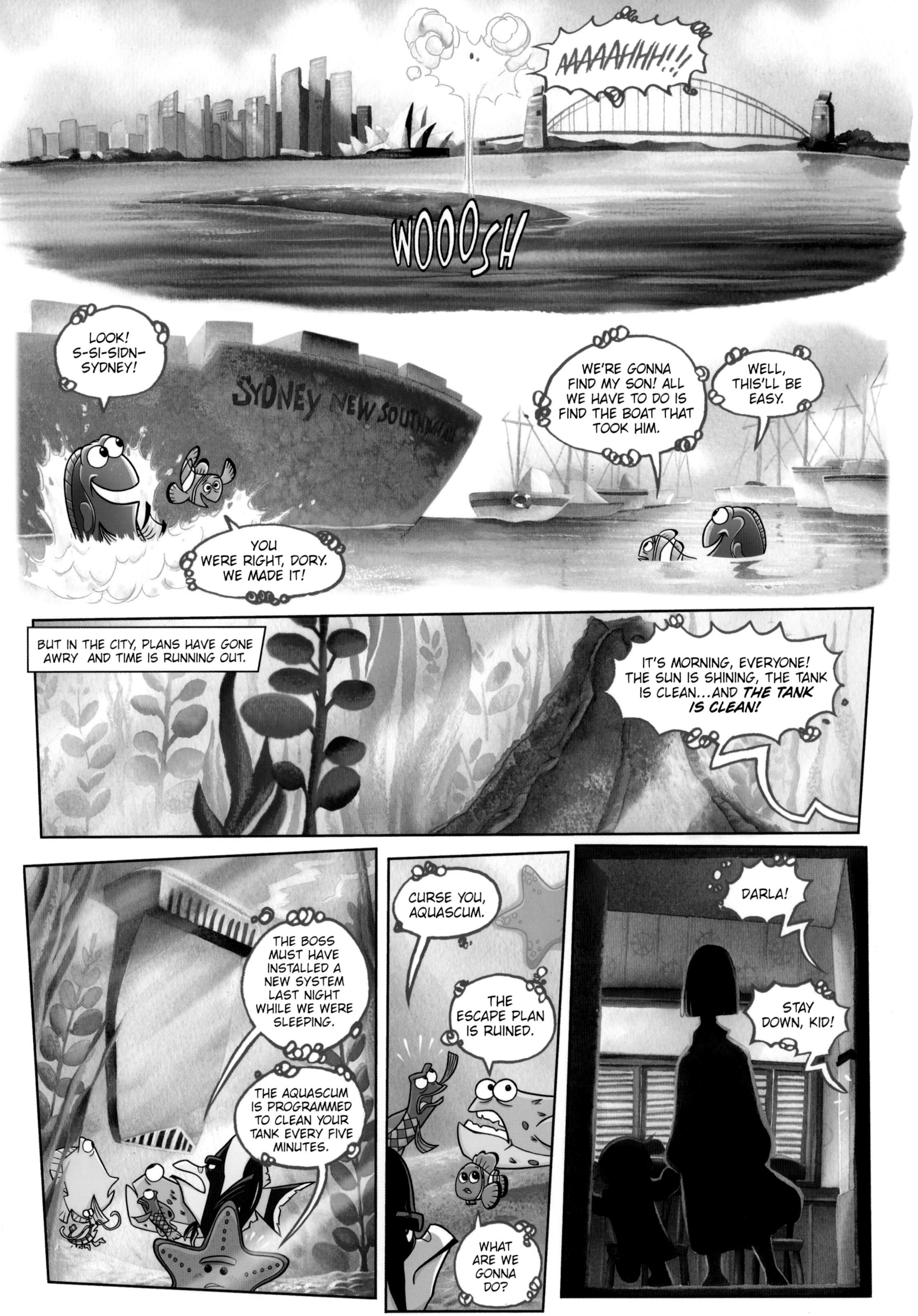
AAAAAHHH!!!
WOOOSH
LOOK! S-SI-SIDN-SYDNEY!
SYDNEY NEW SOUTH
YOU WERE RIGHT, DORY. WE MADE IT!
WE'RE GONNA FIND MY SON! ALL WE HAVE TO DO IS FIND THE BOAT THAT TOOK HIM.
WELL, THIS'LL BE EASY.
BUT IN THE CITY, PLANS HAVE GONE AWRY AND TIME IS RUNNING OUT.
IT'S MORNING, EVERYONE! THE SUN IS SHINING, THE TANK IS CLEAN...AND *THE TANK IS CLEAN!*
THE BOSS MUST HAVE INSTALLED A NEW SYSTEM LAST NIGHT WHILE WE WERE SLEEPING.
THE AQUASCUM IS PROGRAMMED TO CLEAN YOUR TANK EVERY FIVE MINUTES.
CURSE YOU, AQUASCUM.
THE ESCAPE PLAN IS RUINED.
WHAT ARE WE GONNA DO?
DARLA!
STAY DOWN, KID!

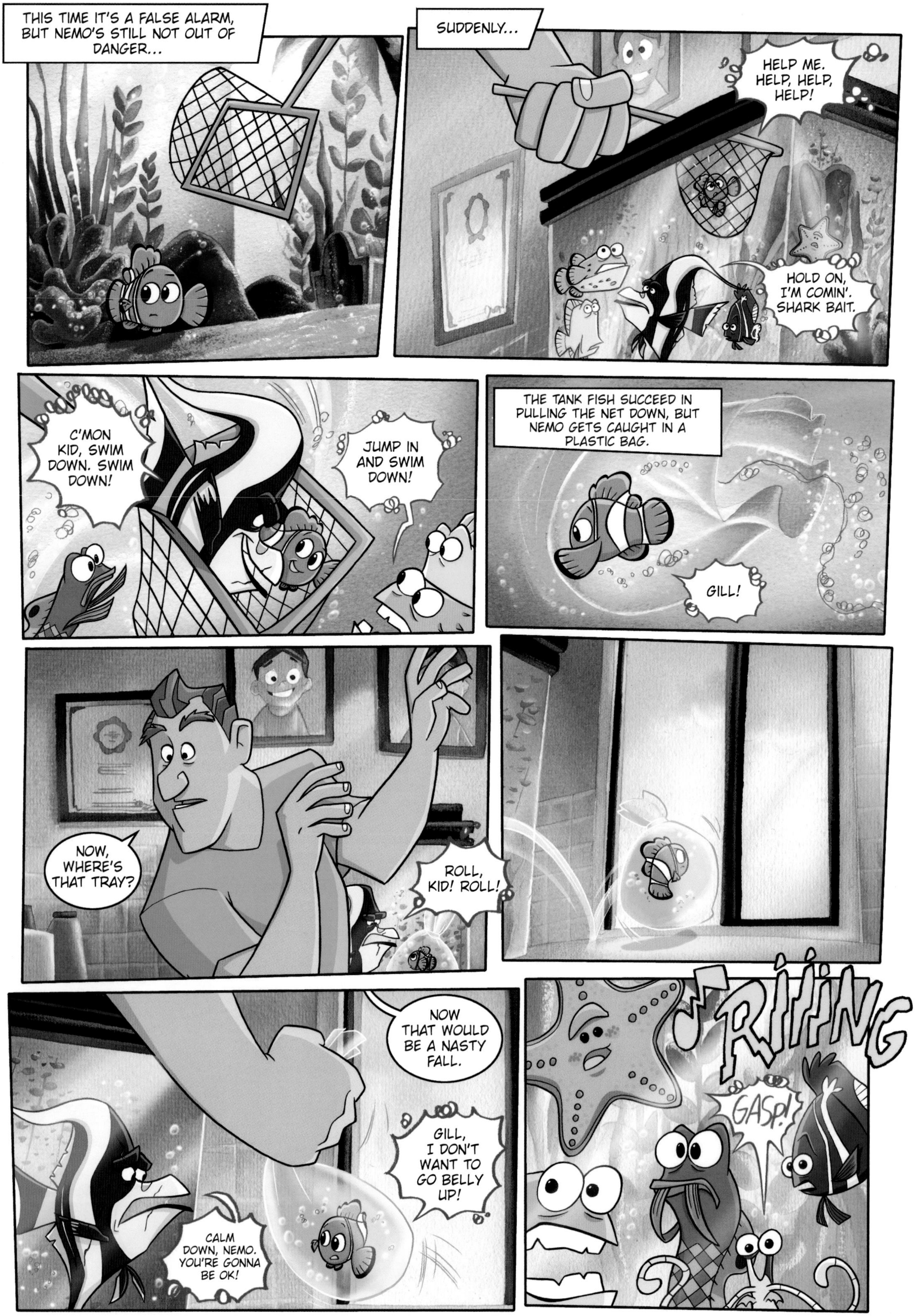
THIS TIME IT'S A FALSE ALARM, BUT NEMO'S STILL NOT OUT OF DANGER...
SUDDENLY...
HELP ME. HELP, HELP, HELP!
HOLD ON, I'M COMIN'. SHARK BAIT.
C'MON KID, SWIM DOWN. SWIM DOWN!
JUMP IN AND SWIM DOWN!
THE TANK FISH SUCCEED IN PULLING THE NET DOWN, BUT NEMO GETS CAUGHT IN A PLASTIC BAG.
GILL!
NOW, WHERE'S THAT TRAY?
ROLL, KID! ROLL!
NOW THAT WOULD BE A NASTY FALL.
GILL, I DON'T WANT TO GO BELLY UP!
CALM DOWN, NEMO. YOU'RE GONNA BE OK!
RIIIING
GASP!

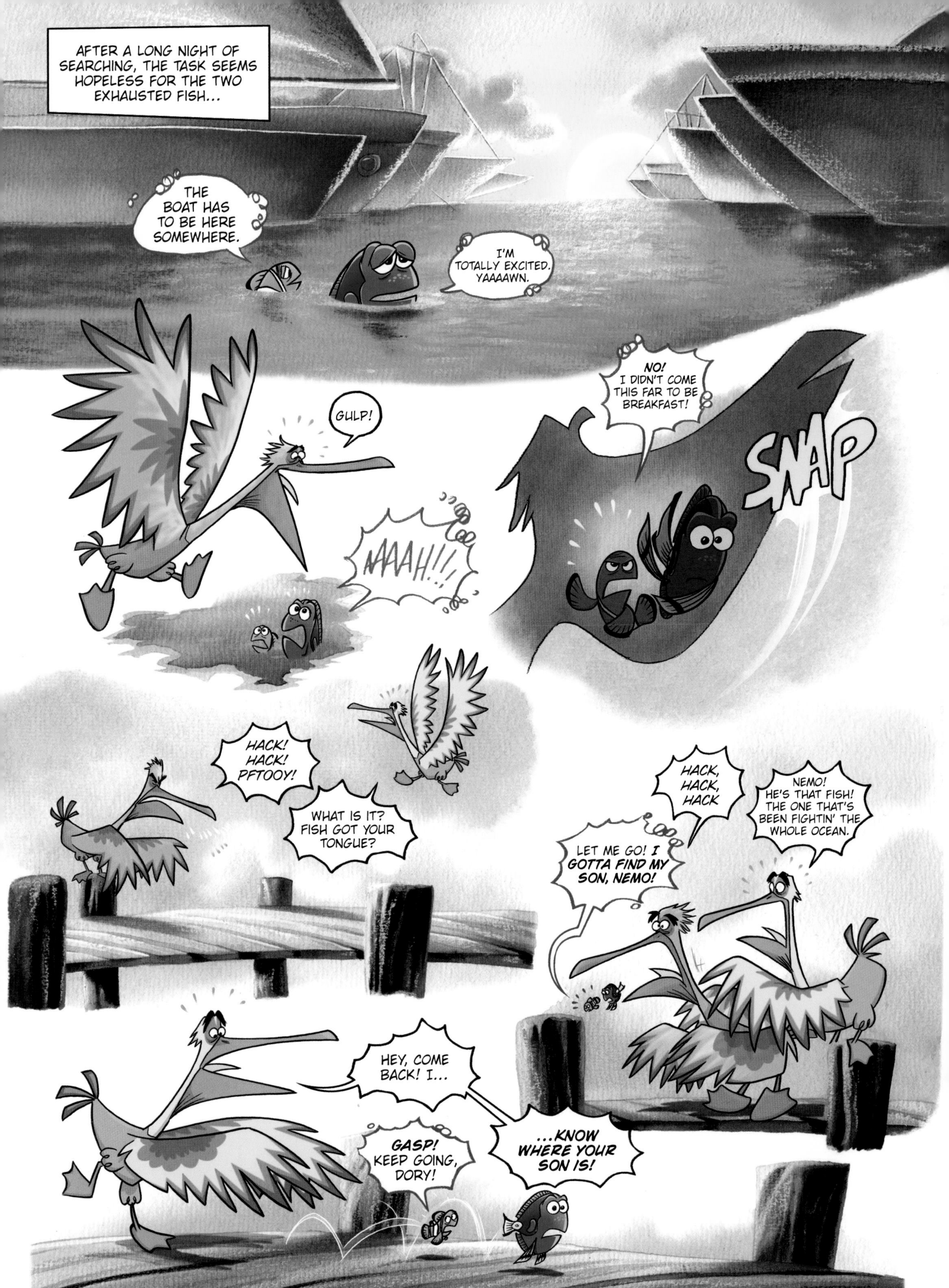
AFTER A LONG NIGHT OF SEARCHING, THE TASK SEEMS HOPELESS FOR THE TWO EXHAUSTED FISH...
THE BOAT HAS TO BE HERE SOMEWHERE.
I'M TOTALLY EXCITED. YAAAAWN.
GULP!
AAAAH!!!
NO! I DIDN'T COME THIS FAR TO BE BREAKFAST!
SNAP
HACK! HACK! PFTOOY!
WHAT IS IT? FISH GOT YOUR TONGUE?
LET ME GO! I GOTTA FIND MY SON, NEMO!
HACK, HACK, HACK
NEMO! HE'S THAT FISH! THE ONE THAT'S BEEN FIGHTIN' THE WHOLE OCEAN.
HEY, COME BACK! I...
...KNOW WHERE YOUR SON IS!
GASP! KEEP GOING, DORY!

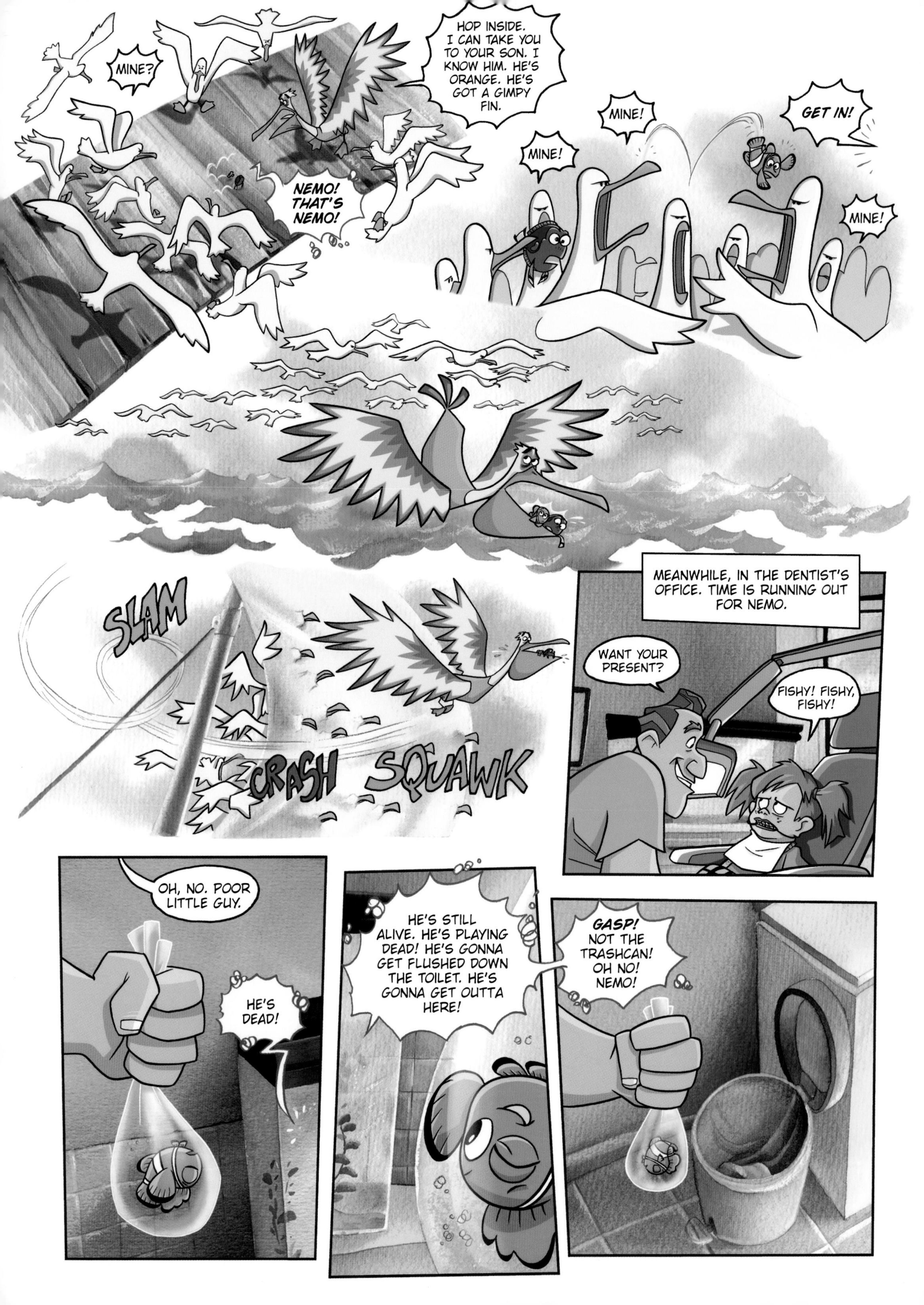
MINE?
HOP INSIDE. I CAN TAKE YOU TO YOUR SON. I KNOW HIM. HE'S ORANGE. HE'S GOT A GIMPY FIN.
NEMO! THAT'S NEMO!
MINE!
MINE!
GET IN!
MINE!
SLAM
CRASH
SQUAWK
MEANWHILE, IN THE DENTIST'S OFFICE. TIME IS RUNNING OUT FOR NEMO.
WANT YOUR PRESENT?
FISHY! FISHY, FISHY!
OH, NO. POOR LITTLE GUY.
HE'S DEAD!
HE'S STILL ALIVE. HE'S PLAYING DEAD! HE'S GONNA GET FLUSHED DOWN THE TOILET. HE'S GONNA GET OUTTA HERE!
GASP! NOT THE TRASHCAN! OH NO! NEMO!

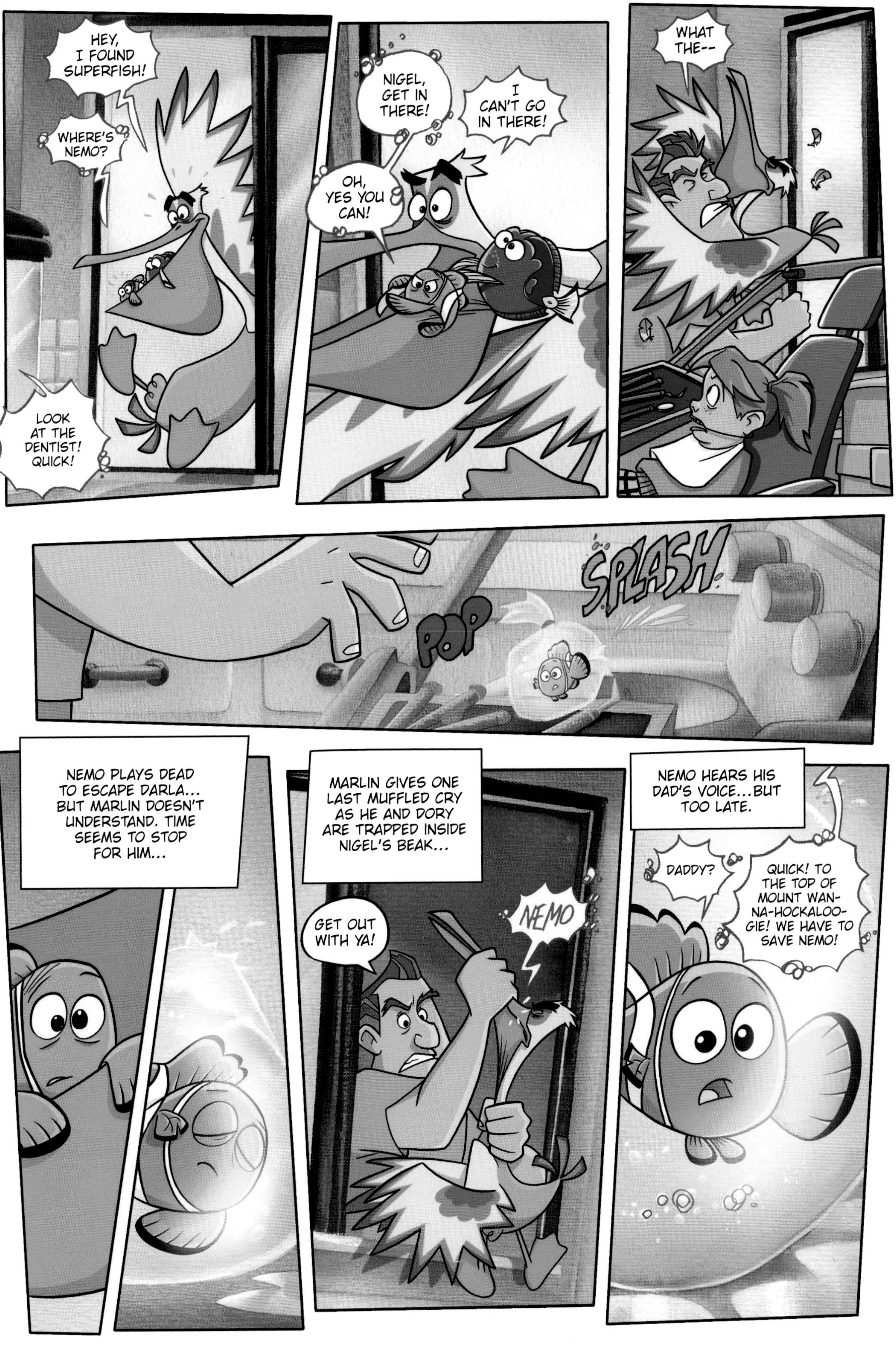
HEY, I FOUND SUPERFISH!
WHERE'S NEMO?
LOOK AT THE DENTIST! QUICK!
NIGEL, GET IN THERE!
I CAN'T GO IN THERE!
OH, YES YOU CAN!
WHAT THE--
SPLASH
POP
NEMO PLAYS DEAD TO ESCAPE DARLA... BUT MARLIN DOESN'T UNDERSTAND. TIME SEEMS TO STOP FOR HIM...
MARLIN GIVES ONE LAST MUFFLED CRY AS HE AND DORY ARE TRAPPED INSIDE NIGEL'S BEAK...
GET OUT WITH YA!
NEMO
NEMO HEARS HIS DAD'S VOICE... BUT TOO LATE.
DADDY?
QUICK! TO THE TOP OF MOUNT WAN-NA-HOCKALOO-GIE! WE HAVE TO SAVE NEMO!

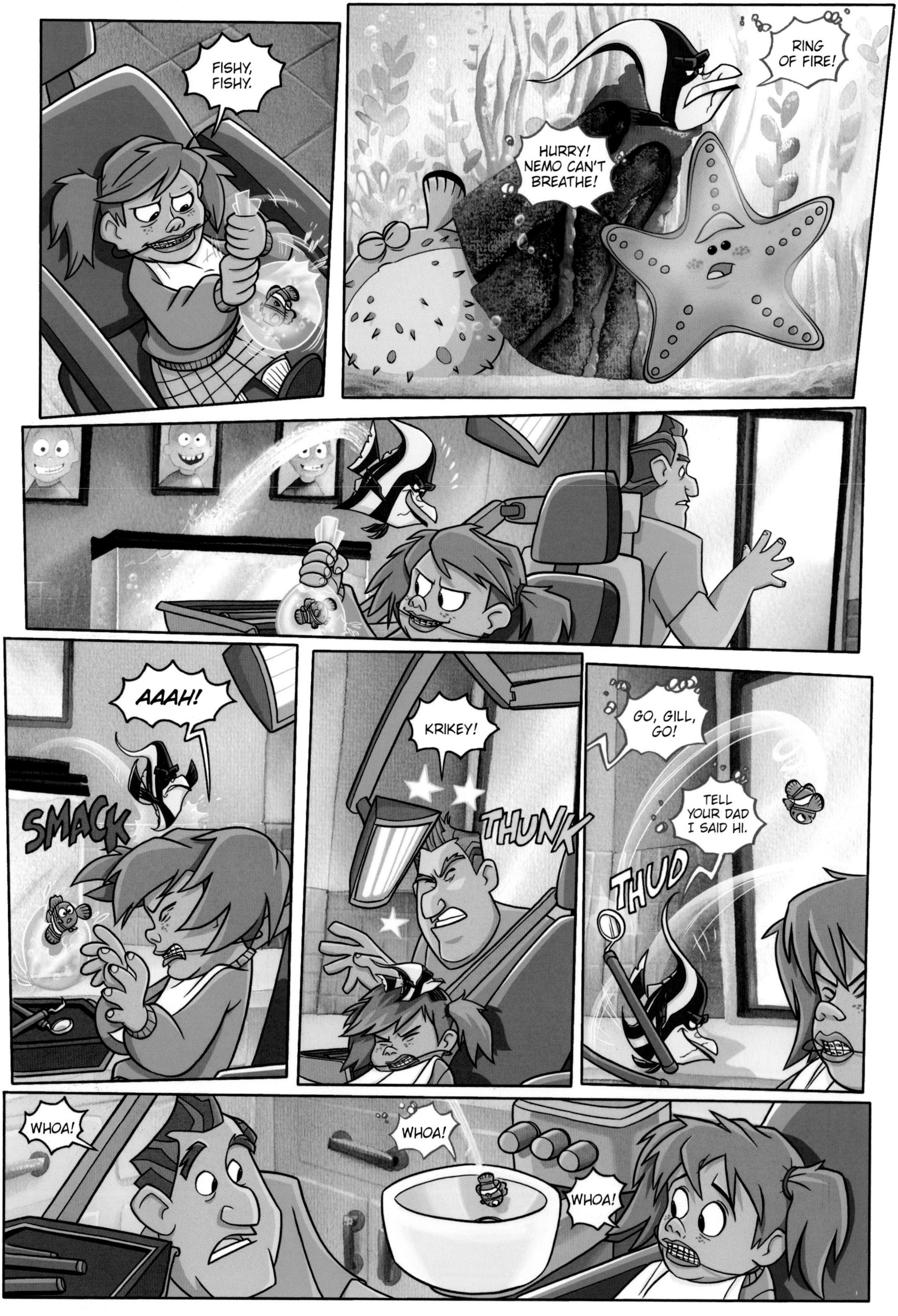
FISHY, FISHY.
RING OF FIRE!
HURRY! NEMO CAN'T BREATHE!
AAAH!
SMACK
KRIKEY!
THUNK
GO, GILL, GO!
TELL YOUR DAD I SAID HI.
THUD
WHOA!
WHOA!
WHOA!

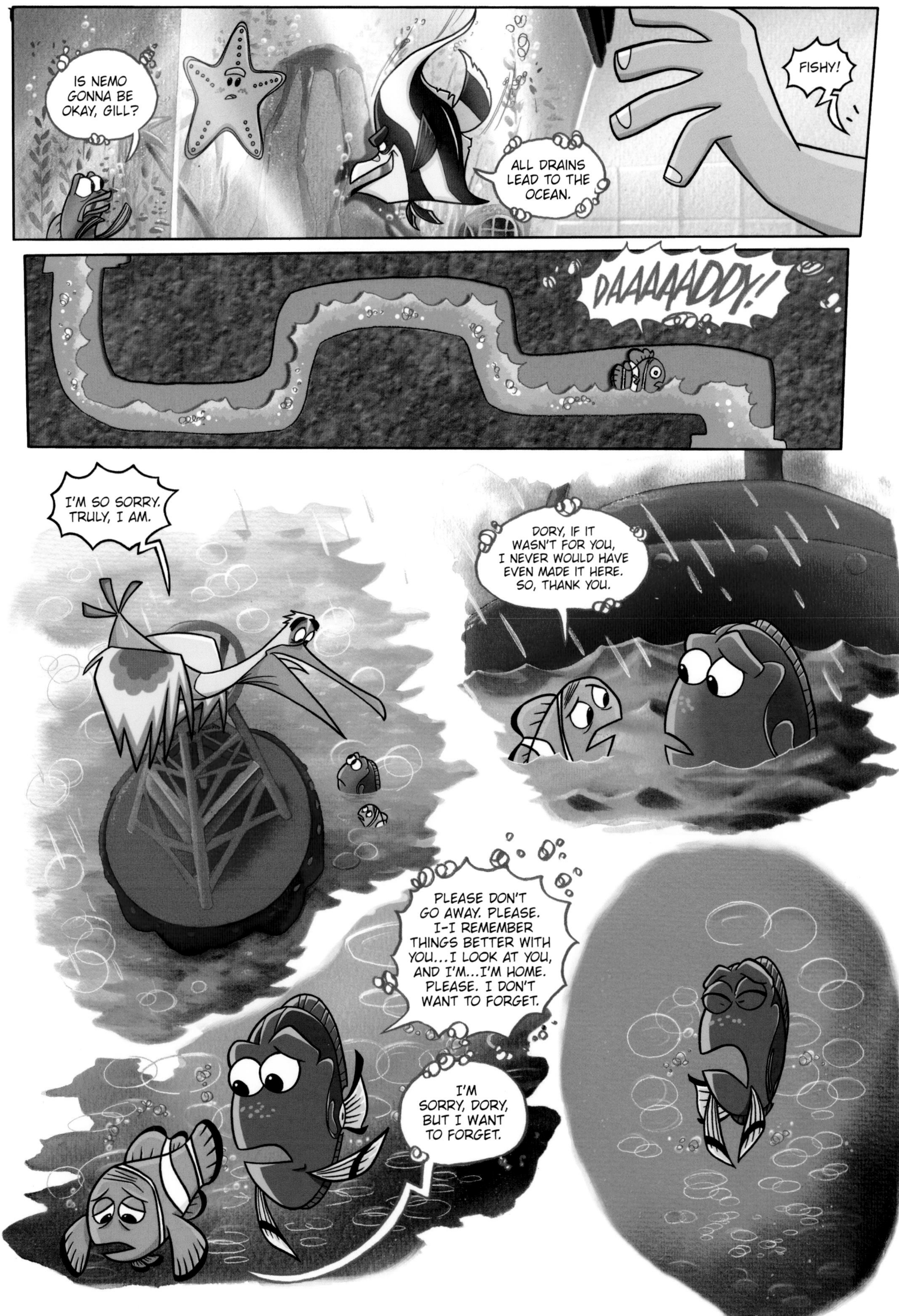
IS NEMO GONNA BE OKAY, GILL?
ALL DRAINS LEAD TO THE OCEAN.
FISHY!
DAAAAADDY!
I'M SO SORRY. TRULY, I AM.
DORY, IF IT WASN'T FOR YOU, I NEVER WOULD HAVE EVEN MADE IT HERE. SO, THANK YOU.
PLEASE DON'T GO AWAY. PLEASE. I-I REMEMBER THINGS BETTER WITH YOU...I LOOK AT YOU, AND I'M...I'M HOME. PLEASE. I DON'T WANT TO FORGET.
I'M SORRY, DORY, BUT I WANT TO FORGET.

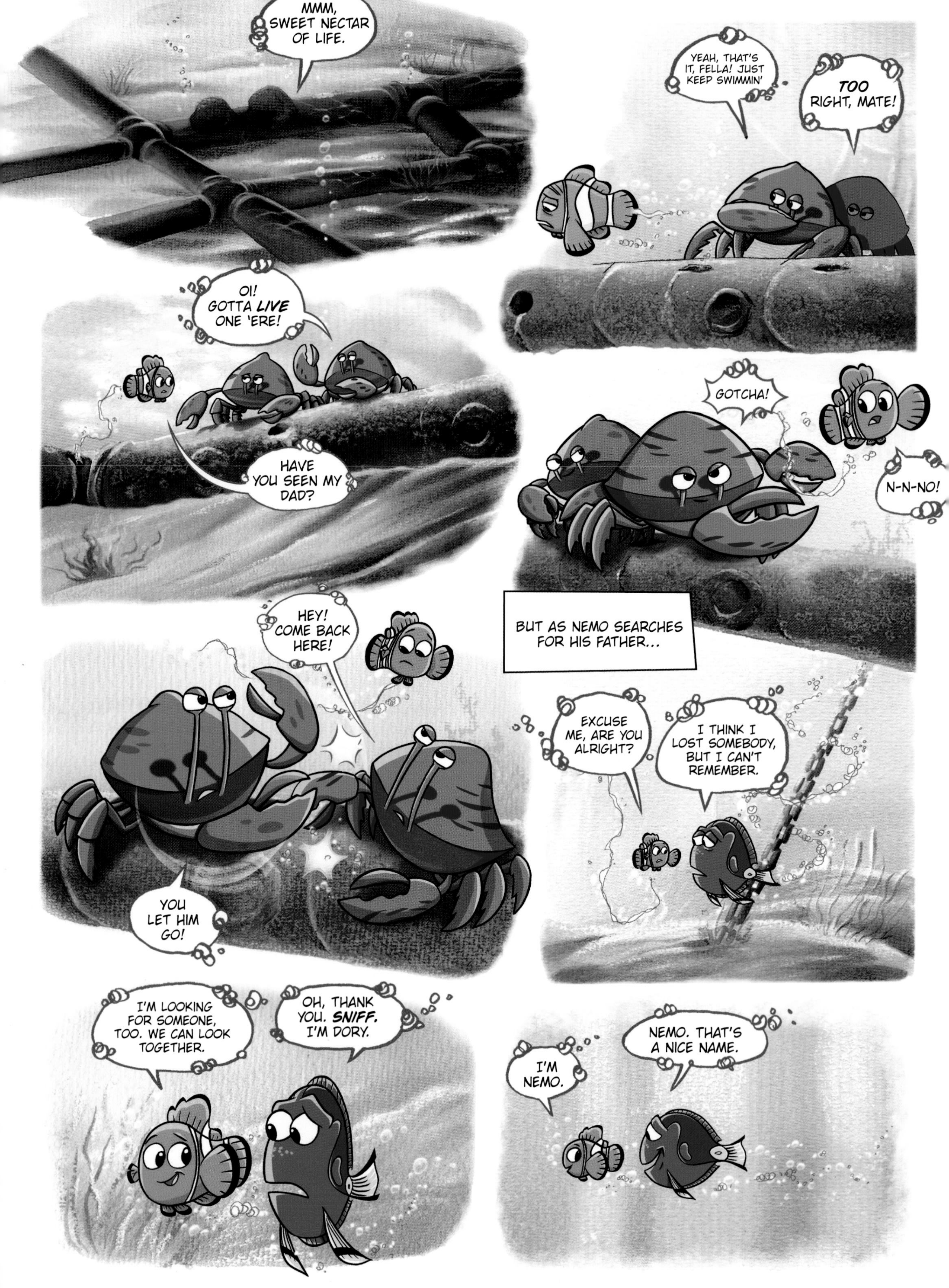

MMM, SWEET NECTAR OF LIFE.
YEAH, THAT'S IT, FELLA! JUST KEEP SWIMMIN'
TOO RIGHT, MATE!
OI! GOTTA LIVE ONE 'ERE!
HAVE YOU SEEN MY DAD?
GOTCHA!
N-N-NO!
HEY! COME BACK HERE!
YOU LET HIM GO!
BUT AS NEMO SEARCHES FOR HIS FATHER...
EXCUSE ME, ARE YOU ALRIGHT?
I THINK I LOST SOMEBODY, BUT I CAN'T REMEMBER.
I'M LOOKING FOR SOMEONE, TOO. WE CAN LOOK TOGETHER.
OH, THANK YOU. SNIFF. I'M DORY.
I'M NEMO.
NEMO. THAT'S A NICE NAME.

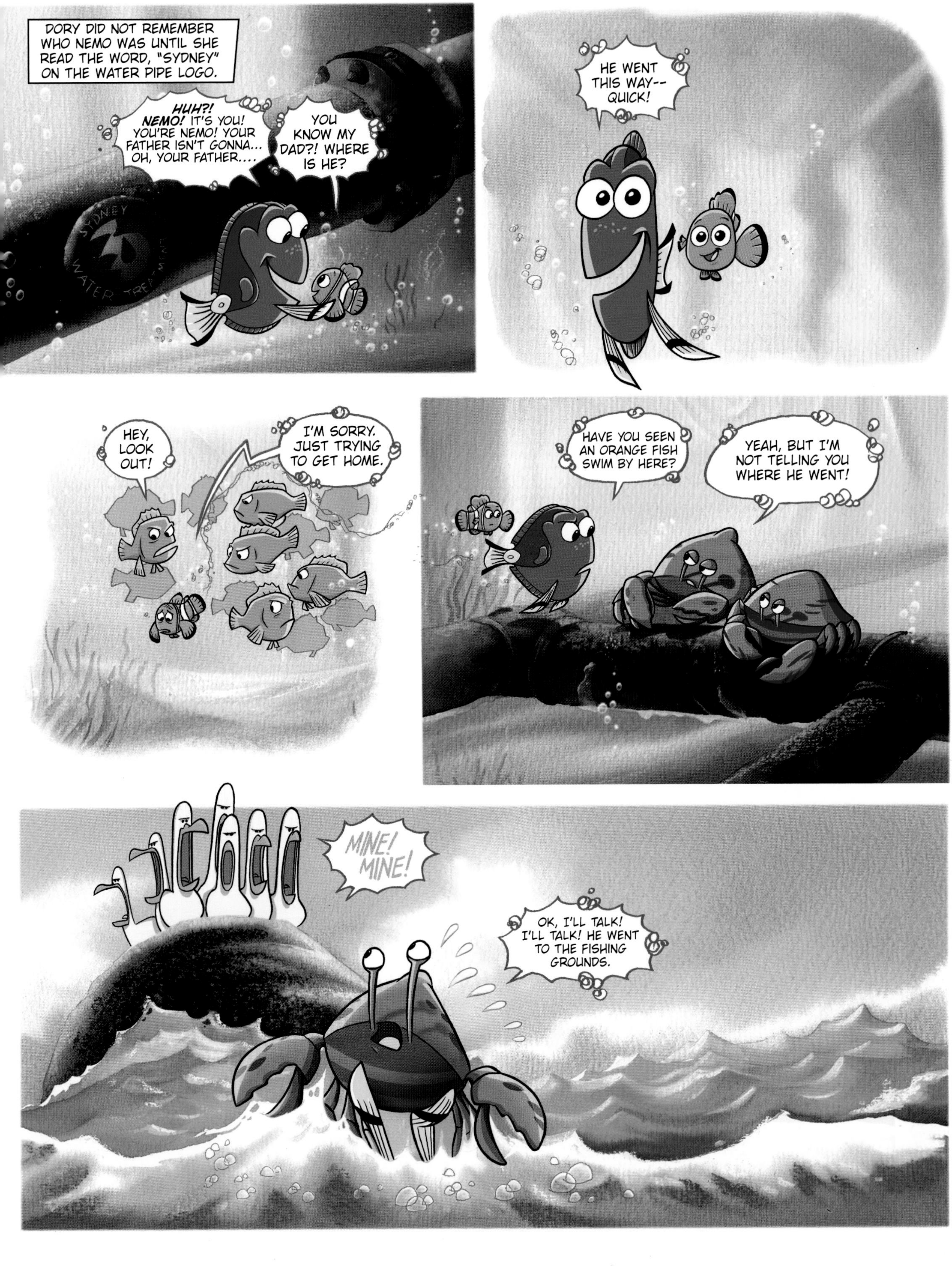
DORY DID NOT REMEMBER WHO NEMO WAS UNTIL SHE READ THE WORD, "SYDNEY" ON THE WATER PIPE LOGO.
HUH?! NEMO! IT'S YOU! YOU'RE NEMO! YOUR FATHER ISN'T GONNA... OH, YOUR FATHER....
YOU KNOW MY DAD?! WHERE IS HE?
SYDNEY WATER TREATMENT
HE WENT THIS WAY-- QUICK!
HEY, LOOK OUT!
I'M SORRY. JUST TRYING TO GET HOME.
HAVE YOU SEEN AN ORANGE FISH SWIM BY HERE?
YEAH, BUT I'M NOT TELLING YOU WHERE HE WENT!
MINE! MINE!
OK, I'LL TALK! I'LL TALK! HE WENT TO THE FISHING GROUNDS.

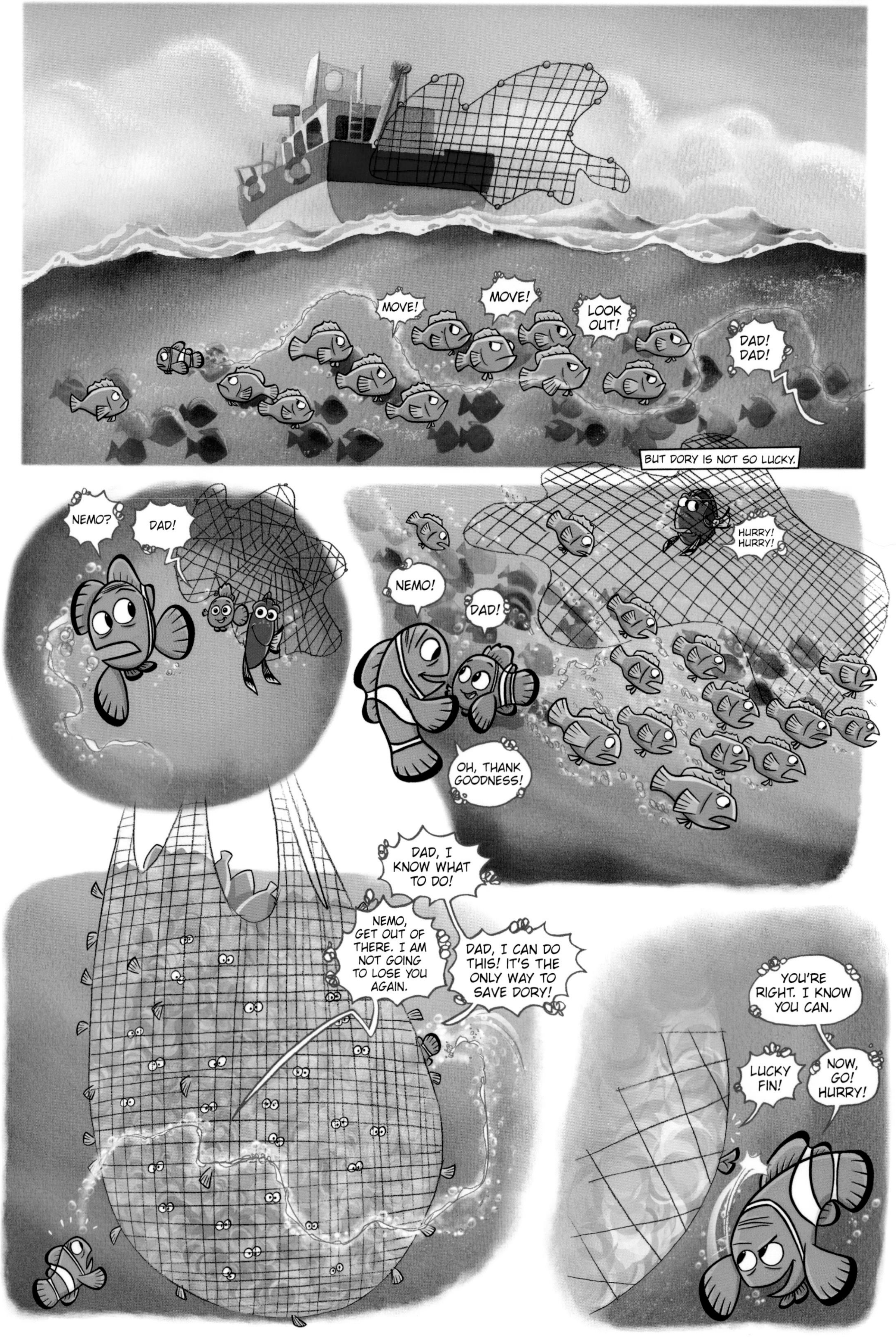
MOVE!
MOVE!
LOOK OUT!
DAD! DAD!
BUT DORY IS NOT SO LUCKY.
NEMO?
DAD!
HURRY! HURRY!
NEMO!
DAD!
OH, THANK GOODNESS!
DAD, I KNOW WHAT TO DO!
NEMO, GET OUT OF THERE. I AM NOT GOING TO LOSE YOU AGAIN.
DAD, I CAN DO THIS! IT'S THE ONLY WAY TO SAVE DORY!
YOU'RE RIGHT. I KNOW YOU CAN.
LUCKY FIN!
NOW, GO! HURRY!

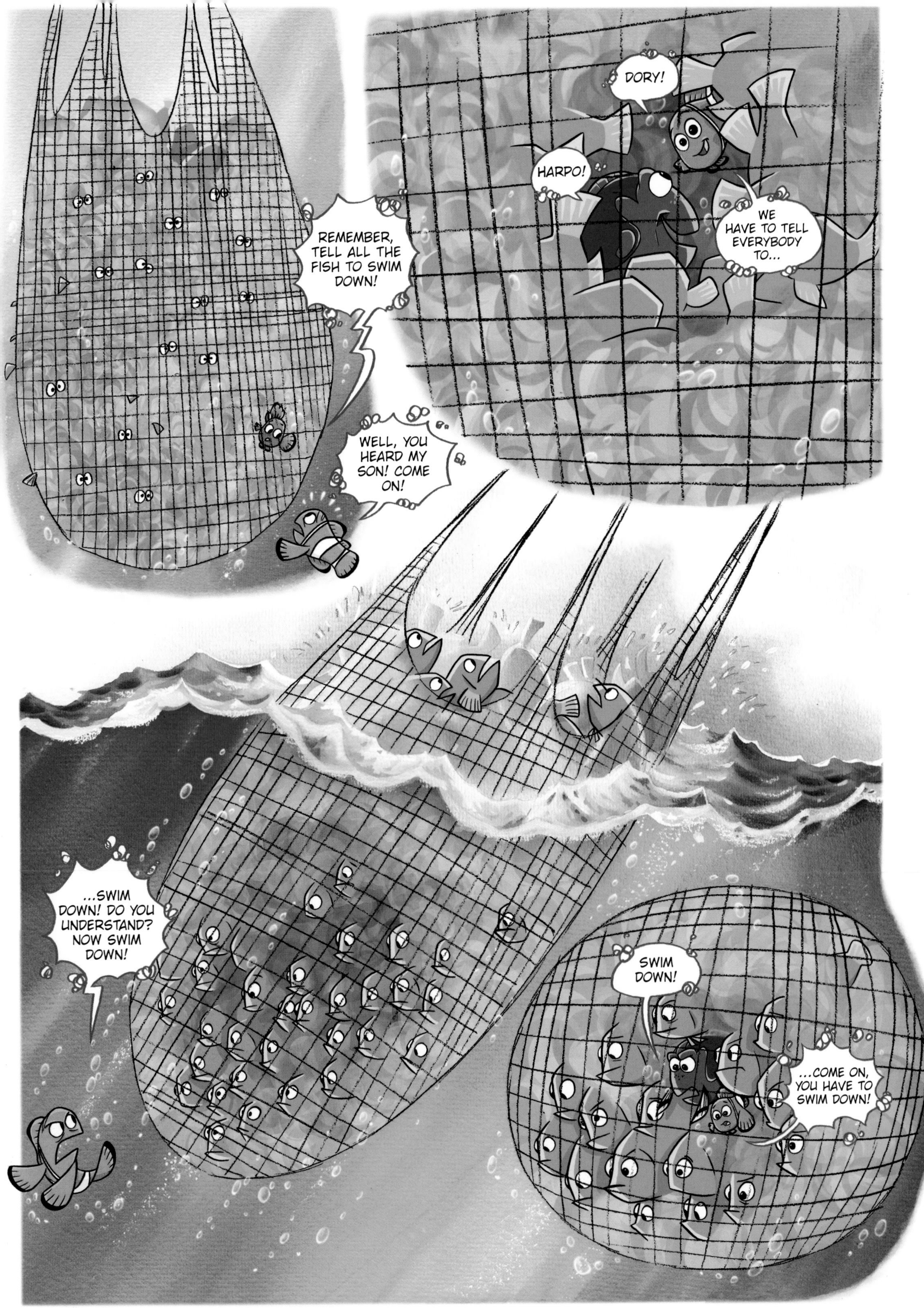

REMEMBER, TELL ALL THE FISH TO SWIM DOWN!
DORY!
HARPO!
WE HAVE TO TELL EVERYBODY TO...
WELL, YOU HEARD MY SON! COME ON!
...SWIM DOWN! DO YOU UNDERSTAND? NOW SWIM DOWN!
SWIM DOWN!
...COME ON, YOU HAVE TO SWIM DOWN!

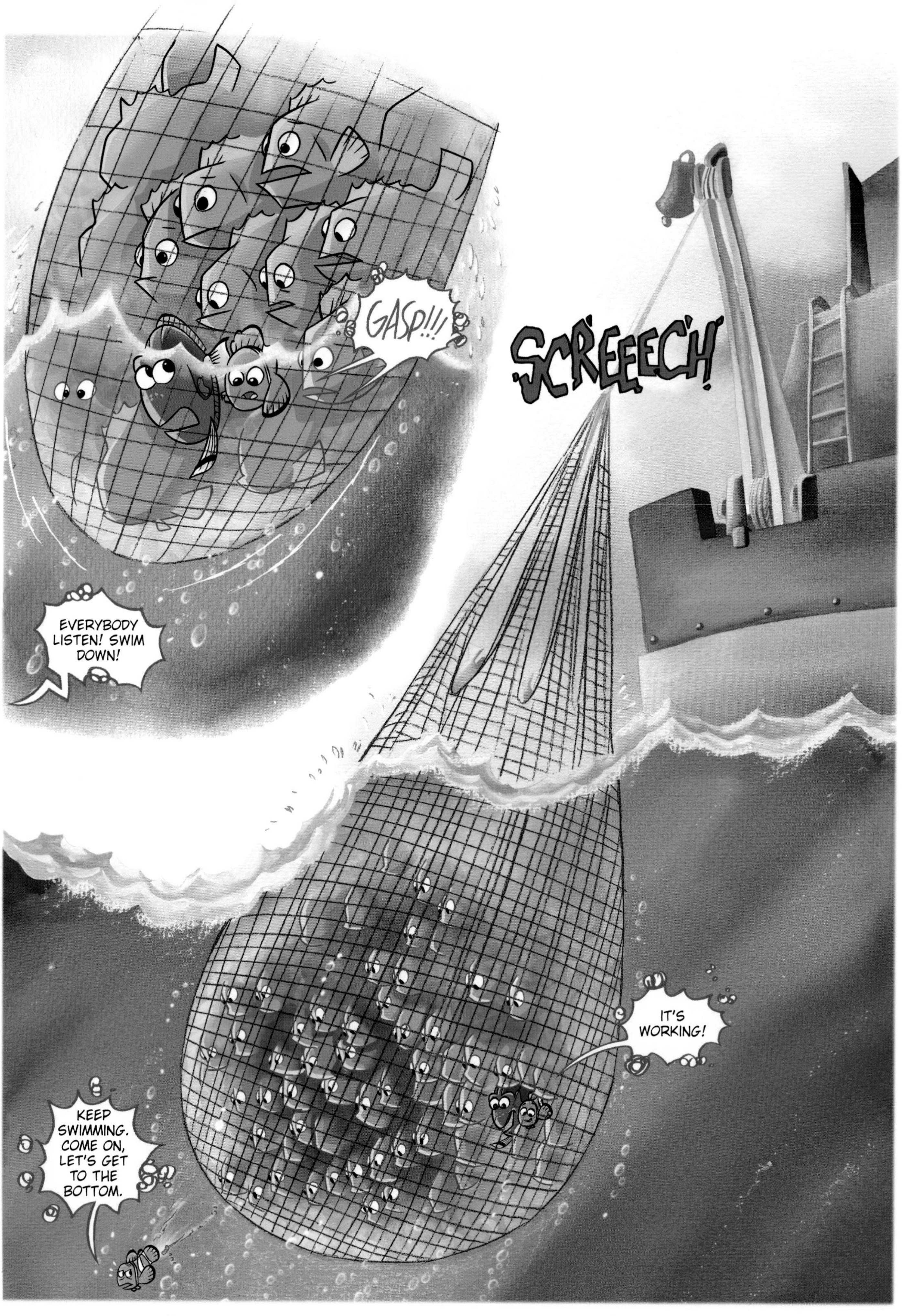
GASP!!!
SCREEECH!
EVERYBODY LISTEN! SWIM DOWN!
IT'S WORKING!
KEEP SWIMMING. COME ON, LET'S GET TO THE BOTTOM.

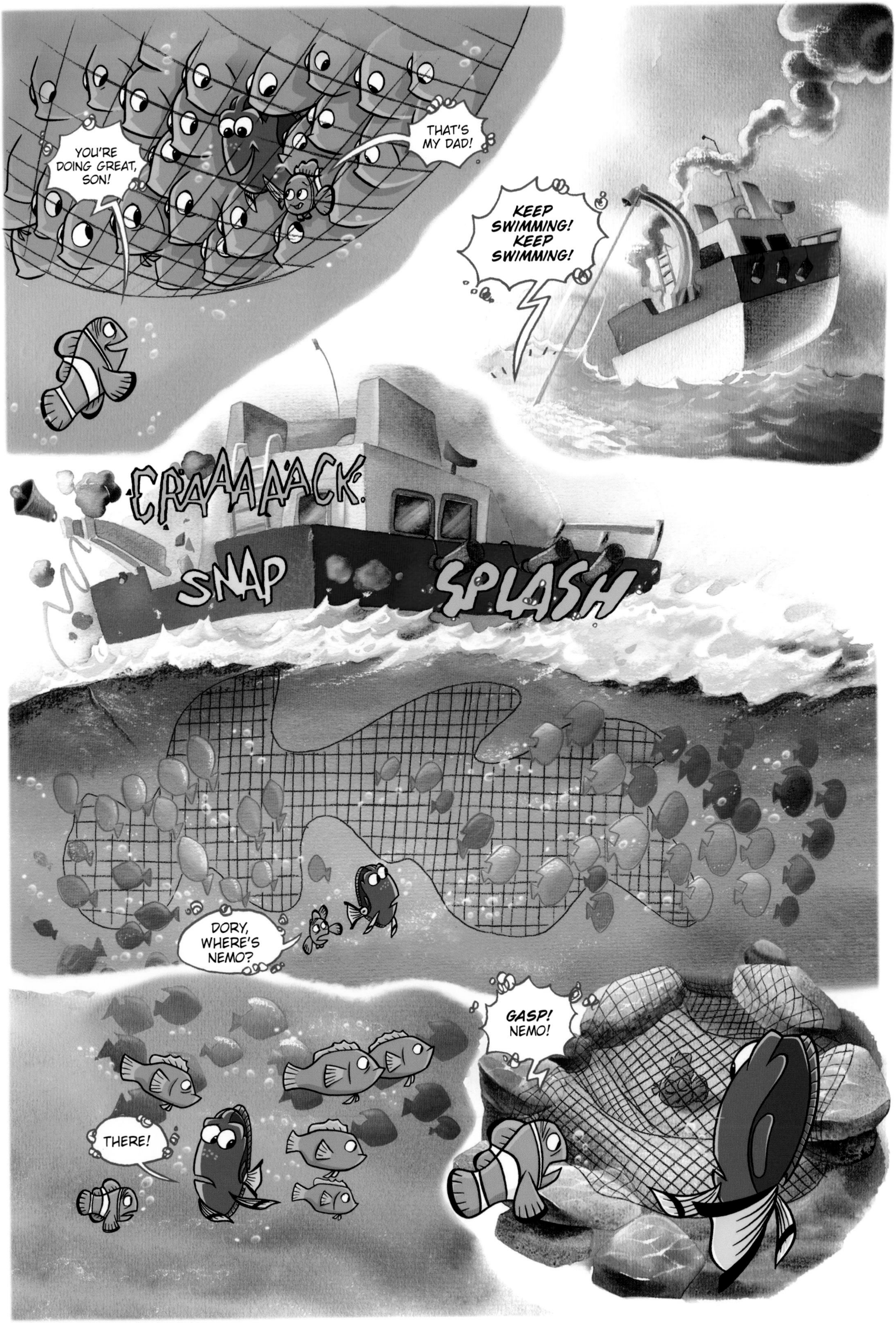
YOU'RE DOING GREAT, SON!
THAT'S MY DAD!
KEEP SWIMMING! KEEP SWIMMING!
CRAAAAACK!
SNAP
SPLASH
DORY, WHERE'S NEMO?
THERE!
GASP! NEMO!

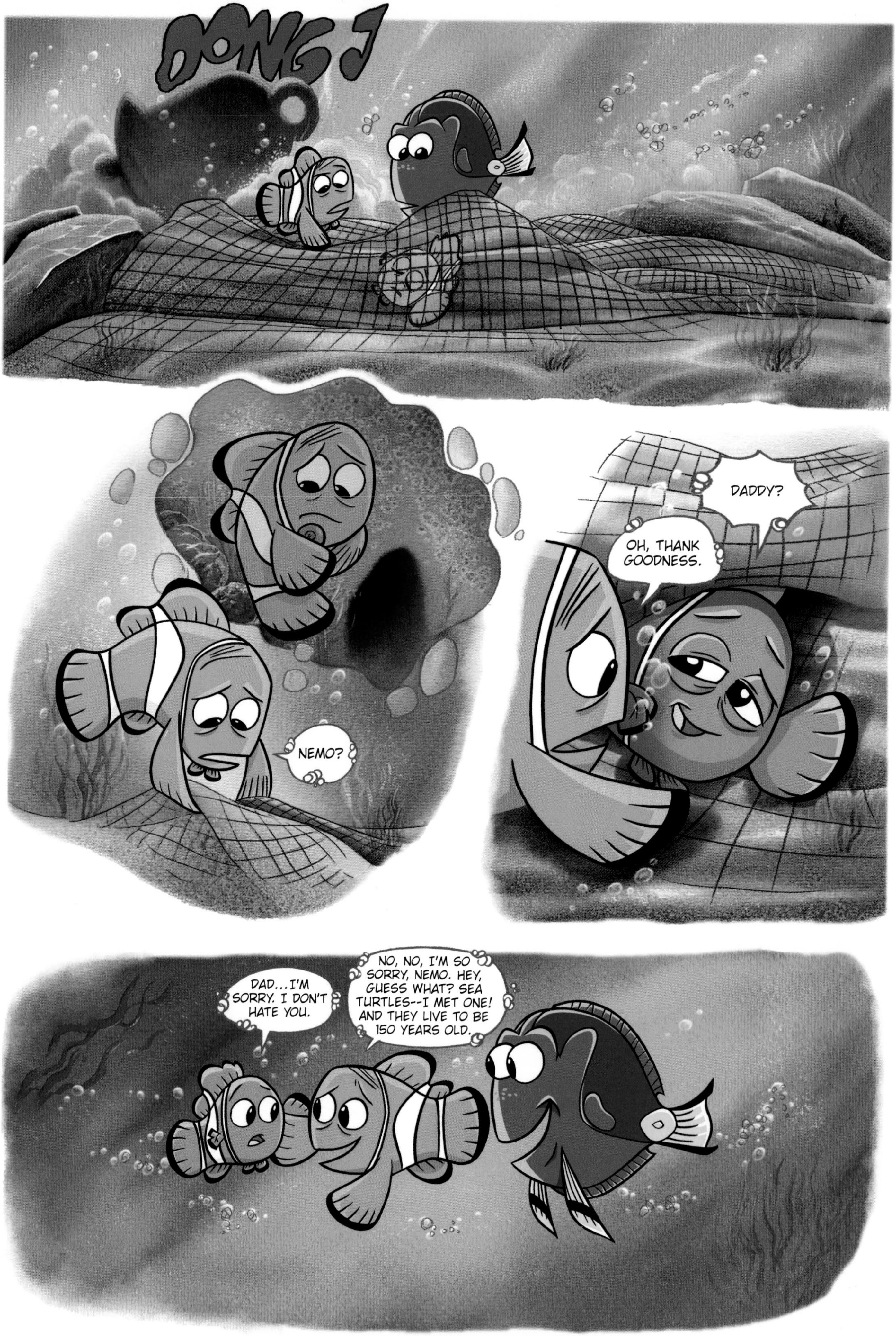
DONG
NEMO?
DADDY?
OH, THANK GOODNESS.
DAD...I'M SORRY. I DON'T HATE YOU.
NO, NO, I'M SO SORRY, NEMO. HEY, GUESS WHAT? SEA TURTLES--I MET ONE! AND THEY LIVE TO BE 150 YEARS OLD.

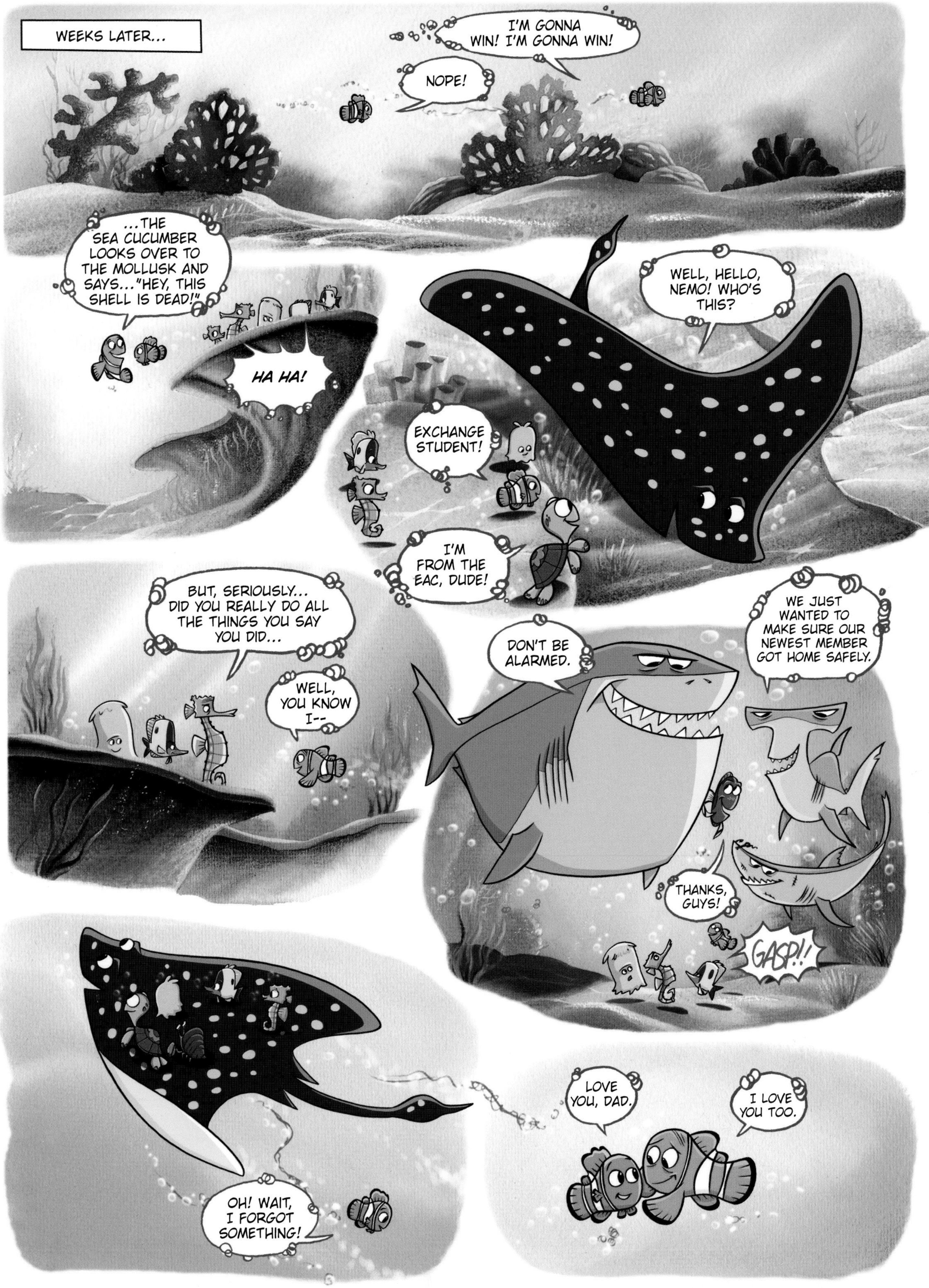

WEEKS LATER...
I'M GONNA WIN! I'M GONNA WIN!
NOPE!
...THE SEA CUCUMBER LOOKS OVER TO THE MOLLUSK AND SAYS..."HEY, THIS SHELL IS DEAD!"
HA HA!
WELL, HELLO, NEMO! WHO'S THIS?
EXCHANGE STUDENT!
I'M FROM THE EAC, DUDE!
BUT, SERIOUSLY... DID YOU REALLY DO ALL THE THINGS YOU SAY YOU DID...
WELL, YOU KNOW I--
DON'T BE ALARMED.
WE JUST WANTED TO MAKE SURE OUR NEWEST MEMBER GOT HOME SAFELY.
THANKS, GUYS!
GASP!!
OH! WAIT, I FORGOT SOMETHING!
LOVE YOU, DAD.
I LOVE YOU TOO.

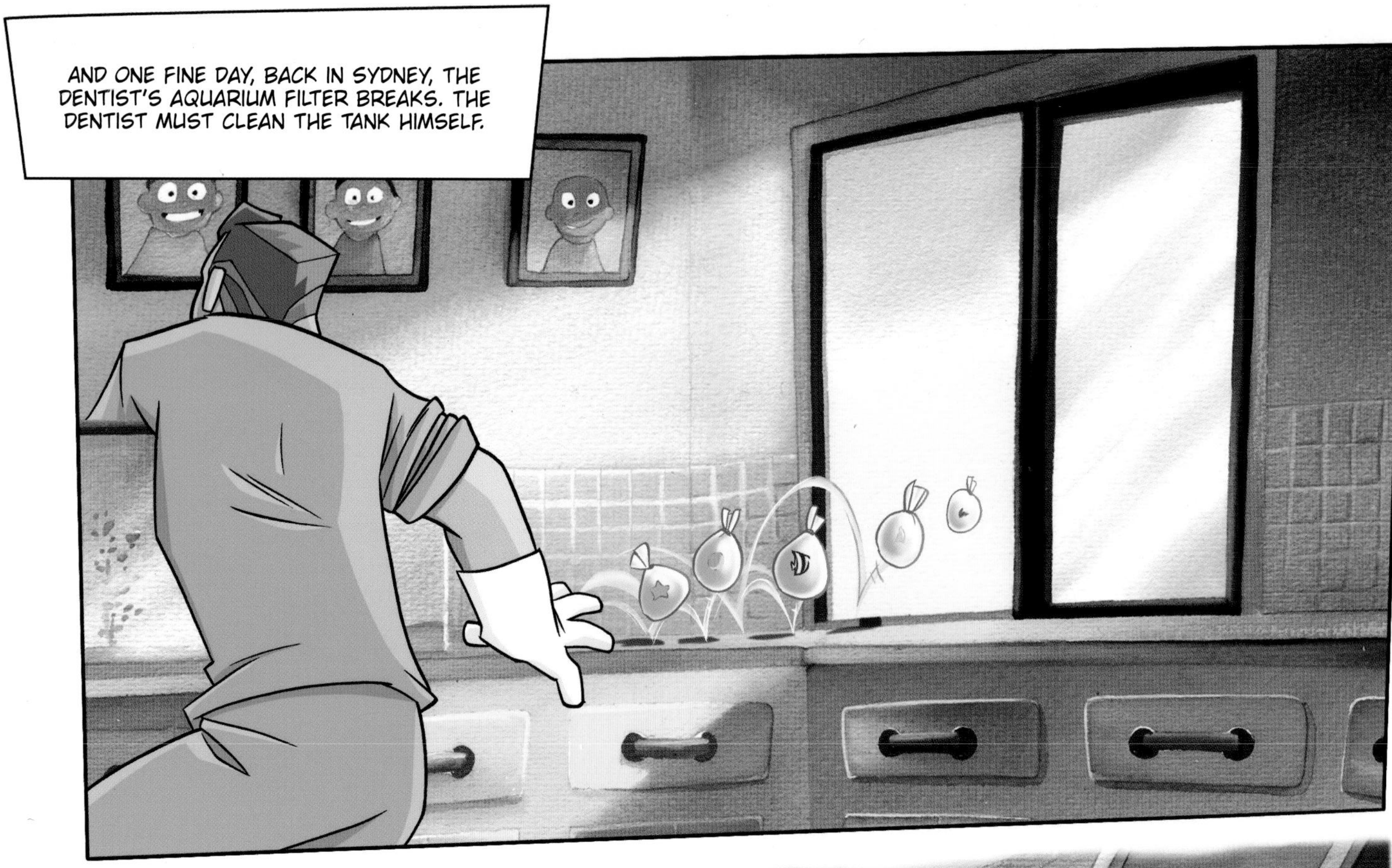
AND ONE FINE DAY, BACK IN SYDNEY, THE DENTIST'S AQUARIUM FILTER BREAKS. THE DENTIST MUST CLEAN THE TANK HIMSELF.

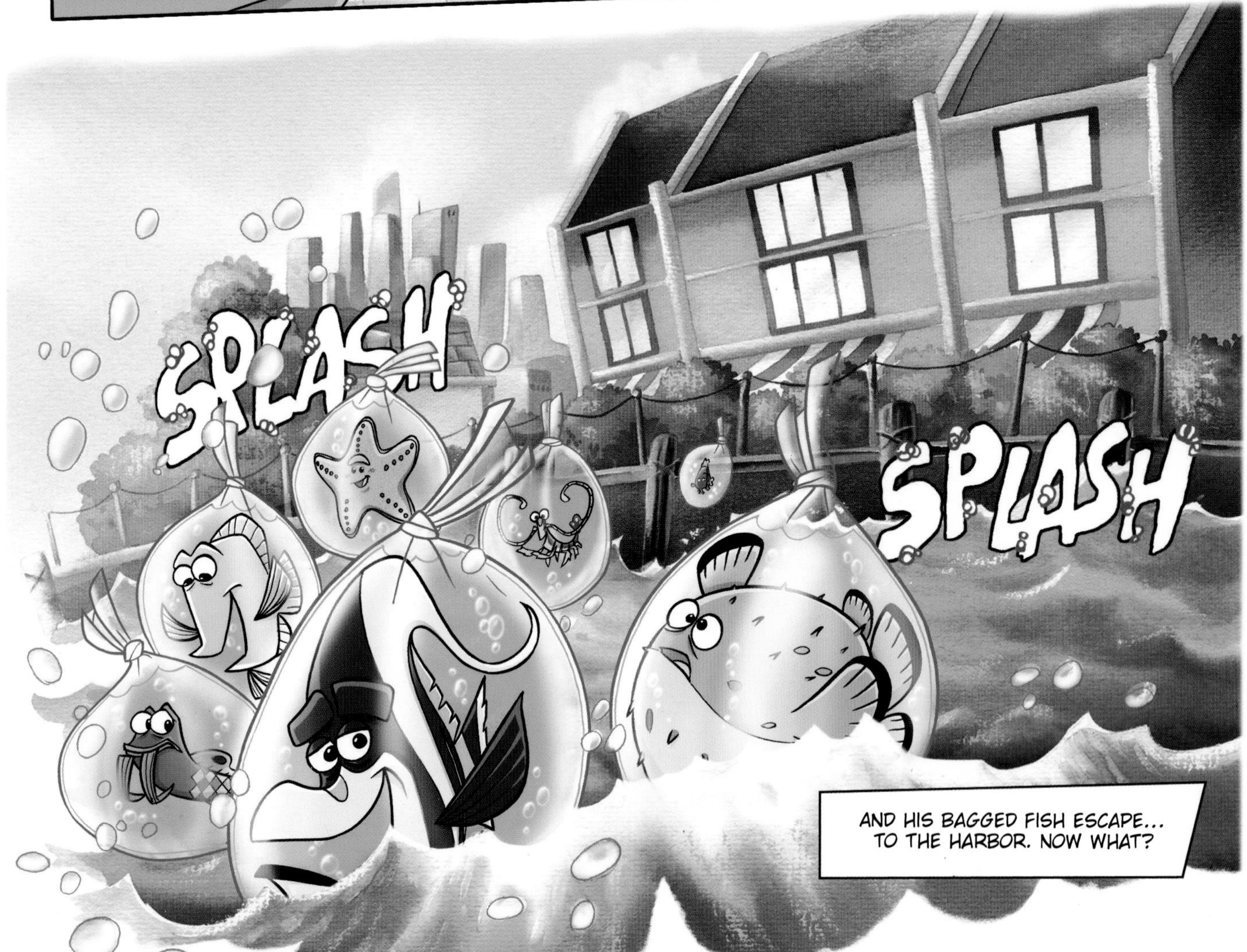
SPLASH
SPLASH
AND HIS BAGGED FISH ESCAPE... TO THE HARBOR. NOW WHAT?

THE END